SASSY COWGIRL KISSES

KATHY FAWCETT

CHAPTER 1

"*T*hirty seven, thirty eight, thirty *nine*," Sassy counted off in a rather boisterous voice. Her shouting didn't bother anybody, since there was no one to hear her. No people, that is.

"Hey, sheep, hold still. I'm almost done."

She hadn't yet counted the one closest to her car, she was saving him for last. Number forty boldly met her stare and answered her yell with a loud *Maaa* of his own. He was the troublemaker; the one that wouldn't give her the courtesy of averting his eyes when she threw off her day clothes under the clear blue sky and slipped into her pink bikini.

And why not?

The day was warm, the sun was high, and not a single car had come by in the two hours she'd been stranded there. The likelihood of somebody catching her in her altogether was slim to none. And the bikini was a welcome change from the denims and khakis she wore to work at the Wyoming ranch where she was interning for the summer.

"Don't judge," she said to number forty as she tied the narrow string around her neck and smoothed on SPF 30—though not in that order. "This whole little interlude is your fault; you came this close to being a lambchop. I might as well soak up some sun while I wait for help."

Sassy laughed to herself at the irony of the situation. Having recently graduated with a degree in accounting, along with certifications in farm and livestock management, it just made sense that inevitably she'd find herself counting sheep.

When she left earlier to enjoy her day off, Sassy figured she was prepared for anything. Freda, her house mate and co-worker, schooled the Midwest-raised Sassy on the perils of mountain roads before they went their separate ways—Freda, to see her family two hours away, and Sassy to go adventuring.

"Out here, even the main roads are stingy with their gas stations," Freda cautioned. "The back roads are downright *withholding*."

Taking Freda at her word, Sassy made one of her trademark lists before heading out.

Ten gallons of gas in the car.
Twelve bottles of drinking water in a cooler.
One each: a phone charger and a chicken sandwich.
Two running shoes.

This last item may have seemed unnecessary to write down, but she actually showed up for college track once with only one running shoe in her backpack. It was not her finest moment.

Under her miscellaneous column, Sassy wrote *beach bag*, which was stuffed in her trunk and meticulously packed with a towel, bathing suit, sunscreen and a first-aid kit. Lastly, there was one folding chair for napping in the sun, or just sitting quietly with her camera.

By her calculations, the young accountant figured she had been ready for anything.

Anything, that is, except a herd of sheep in the road as she came around a blind curve. She had no choice but to swerve off into a big rock where her little car remained—tire as flat as a pancake. Sassy could change a tire, her daddy had seen to that, but not when it was jammed tight against a boulder, in a field of prickly sagebrush.

Considering the complete lack of cell phone reception, Sassy was in a pickle.

She was not prepared for the *unknown factor*, as her fellow accountants called a missing quotient. It was her least favorite part of number crunching, knowing that she couldn't always see what was ahead. But if accounting didn't teach her that, life certainly did. This past year, especially.

Not a single car had travelled down the road since Sassy found herself stranded. It was the heat of the afternoon, so eventually she changed into her bathing suit, in full view of the nosey sheep. Rejecting the folding chair, she spread the beach towel up the back window of the car so she could stretch out while she waited.

It was too soon to panic, and too far to jog to town—although she might need to before the day was over.

"Just stay put," her parents told her, when she was afraid of being separated as a little girl. "Help will find you." So far, *help* was taking its sweet time in this laid-back wasteland of a state.

Sassy never thought she'd see the day when the cornfields back home, the claustrophobic growth crowding every road for miles and days, would seem like civilization. Wyoming brought a whole new meaning to the word isolation.

The sheep were no help at all.

"Don't you guys know a shepherd or something—someone with two legs and a truck?" Sassy looked over to ask the curious sheep.

Maaa maaa, they answered. *You were driving too faaast around the corner.*

"Thanks for nothing," she said, but knew they might be right.

Eyes closed, she snoozed in the warmth, taking the time to dial the emergency tow truck number in West Gorge every so often, only to see the call fail to connect. Worst case scenario, Sassy figured, she wouldn't return to her rental house tonight, or to work in the morning. Then Freda might put two and two together and send out a search party.

She smiled at the image of a helicopter flying overhead, spotting her lounging in a pink bikini on her rear window. Her eyes quickly closed behind her sunglasses as she nodded off in the sun. It had been a tiring week of early days at West Ranch. Before long, Sassy found herself dreaming of being rescued by a gleaming tow truck, driven by a shining knight. She could almost hear the engine. It sounded so real as it got closer and closer.

Wha...?

Opening her eyes, Sassy realized she wasn't dreaming. The truck was real and coming around the corner—fast. When it screeched to a hard stop, right next to twice-lucky number forty, a tall young man slowly got out and stood in the road.

Wasting no time, she sat up and blinked several times, clearing the sleep from her eyes so she could quickly assess her rescue vehicle, and more importantly, its driver.

CHAPTER 2

"*D*ad, I'm almost home. An hour at the outside, unless I run into traffic on Mount Gander Road—*ha ha.* Can't wait to see you all."

Ash West was parked on the side of the highway, shouting into his phone over the rumble of his truck engine, as his dad's number went to voicemail. Not surprising; Ash was in a part of Wyoming where cell reception was scant—one reason he was calling with an update while his phone still showed bars.

He'd left the freeway a few hours before, and was about to turn off the two-lane highway and onto the semi-paved Mount Gander Road, which would lead into West Gorge. With the red clay bluffs on one side, and boulders the size of houses sitting in a sagebrush field on the other side, cell reception would only get worse before it got better.

Sometimes, if the wind wasn't blowing; if birds weren't perched on the wire and he tapped his boots together three times while making a wish, a call would go through. But he didn't want Ridge worrying about him, so played it safe.

Ash smiled and put his phone in the center console, then put his truck into drive once again. It had been a long few days of driving, and he was so close to home. He was sick of fast food and tired of his own company. Ash had a houseful of family waiting to see him, and no doubt, a refrigerator full of his favorite foods. BBQ pork sandwiches from Red's and Liu's famous spring rolls.

Maybe even a chocolate cake from Cindy's Diner—a man could dream.

Driving along, the windows were down on his truck so he could smell the wildflowers and the pine trees. The sweet air had been washed clean in last night's rain. He was following the mountain range to West Gorge, Wyoming.

Thunk. Thunk.

Every time the truck hit a rock or bump, the boxes in the back would come down hard. They were stuffed with four years of textbooks, Michigan State University sweatshirts and a diploma with the ink still drying.

His honors cords were in there somewhere.

The mountain peaks, Ash noticed, drew closer and became more pronounced as the sun moved high in the sky, then started to dip. A creek alongside the road widened, flowing steadily with icy water that had been snow on the mountain tops just days before. The road went from flat to gentle swells, to up-and-down hills and curves that gave zero visibility as to what was on the other side or around a bend.

"A ribbon of a highway," Ash said out loud to stay alert. It was a line from an old song Granny used to sing, warble really, called *This Land is Your Land.*

As I was walking that ribbon of a highway,
I saw above me an endless skyway,
I saw below me a golden valley,
This land was made for you and me.

Since he was a boy, he thought of that song every time he travelled down a road with the hills and swells; a road that reminded him of ribbon candy on a Christmas tree.

Ash hadn't passed a car in a long time—Mt. Gander Road, he knew, was mostly known by locals and rarely travelled. It didn't show up on every map. That's why it was surprising to come around a bend and see a car half on and half off the road.

"Whooooaaa," he said in surprise, breaking hard. Ash could have swerved around the car, but not the herd of wooly sheep stretched leisurely across both lanes. It appeared they forgot which way they were heading. Sheep, Ash knew, were not that bright.

Ash was even more surprised to see a girl sunbathing and sleeping on the back of the car, wearing a tiny pink swimsuit. As he put the truck in park, she jerked awake, and quickly jumped off. Placing her hand on the car door as if about to hop in, she eyed him warily. It was then he noticed that her front bumper was firmly planted in a rock. A boulder almost as big as her car.

"Hey," Ash said as he stepped out onto the road. Casually, he lifted his arms in the air for a stretch.

"Hey," she shrugged, her voice still gravelly from her interrupted nap.

"Can I help you?" Ash gestured to her car.

"You can call me a tow truck," she said, obviously in a bind.

"Okay, you're a *tow truck*," Ash said, without receiving the laugh he would have gotten back at school, where all the girls thought he was just the funniest thing ever.

"Wow, okay," she said, not impressed.

"Naw, I'm sorry," Ash attempted. "I'm just punchy from driving too long."

The girl nodded again, but remained by her car with the door opened. She wanted a quick escape from the idiot comedian on the desolate road, Ash realized.

"I'll try my phone, but the reception here isn't the best."

"No fooling."

She wasn't cutting him any slack, and why should she? The girl, he

7

could see, was more stunning than any of the Michigan beauties he'd left behind, with her golden hair and long tanned legs. And she was in a predicament—probably waiting for help for a long time.

"If the call doesn't go through, I'll give you a lift into town."

Which would be mighty nice for me, he thought.

Judging by the girl's face, she didn't agree.

Reaching into his truck, Ash retrieved his phone and pulled it out slowly, so as not to startle her. But his hands were suddenly sweaty, making the phone as precarious as a slippery fish—it flipped and flopped in his hands until it smashed onto the road.

The beautiful girl smiled indulgently. Her hair moved around her neck and shoulders in thick buttery waves as the breeze kicked up. She reached up to pull a tendril from her eyes and Ash felt his legs go weak. He couldn't imagine who she was or why she was in West Gorge. He doubted she'd tell him if he asked.

So he didn't.

"Got the phone," Ash said nervously, "now let's see... I have the number for Tig's Tow here somewhere... hey, it's ringing!"

A few minutes later, he hung up and told the girl that Tig and her tow truck would be there soon, and he'd wait with her.

"There's no need for that," she said as she exhaled with relief. "I'll be fine."

"I'm not leaving you alone," he said. "I'll stay right here in my truck, then follow you into town and make sure you're okay."

"That's not necessary," she said again, looking happier than when he'd arrived.

"Well it is," Ash said, "because that's where I'm heading. To West Gorge."

The girl took this in and nodded again.

"I just don't want you to think I'm all alone."

Ash was anxious to go—he hadn't been home since Christmas, and could hardly wait to walk into the ranch house and see his family. If she had somebody, he wouldn't feel guilty about leaving. But looking through her back windshield, the car was empty.

"You can clearly see," the girl said with mischief in her voice and a twinkle in her clear eyes, "that I have forty of my closest friends with me." She gestured towards the herd of sheep, now so at home on the road that Ash thought they might set up camp and stay for a while.

"Well, Bo Peep," Ash said with a laugh, "I stand corrected. But I think we need to help move your friends off the road, or Tig won't be able to get her truck to your car."

"And neither of us will get to West Gorge," she said.

"True. Looks like you have three choices, Bo," he said, making a show of holding up his fingers and counting them off. "*One,* you can stand there and watch me try my hand at shepherding for the first time, or *two,* you can help me."

"What's my third choice?" she asked.

"Sit in your car and lock the door tight, just in case I'm a raving lunatic."

The girl smiled, and her entire face lit up like a Christmas tree, Ash thought.

"I choose number one—I'll stand here and watch you work."

CHAPTER 3

*R*iding in Tig's truck back to town, Sassy looked out the window and privately recalled the boy's face. Seeing how Tig was using the speaker in her truck to talk to her mechanic, pleasantries were not required.

Her mysterious shepherd was *gorgeous*—and a gentleman, Sassy had to admit. Even while trying to keep the flock from loitering in the middle of the road. He didn't leer at her in her bathing suit, or stare while she added a layer of clothes.

She liked the way he turned his tanned face away, but not before flashing a hint of a smile. He was amused by the predicament, she could see, but also bashful. It was refreshing and slightly disarming. She might have felt comfortable enough to ride in his truck, and may have if he'd asked a second time.

Freda talked about cowboys as if they all adhered to a code of honor, but Sassy wasn't willing to accept this as the gospel truth.

"That's a broad paint brush," she told her roommate skeptically. However, this young cowboy could very well be one of the good ones.

But she didn't travel all the way from Illinois to Wyoming for cowboys. They were just an oddity to Sassy, like buffalo grazing along the road, or herds of antelope bouncing among the rocky sagebrush.

The men and the wildlife were trying to figure her out, too, she noticed.

Good luck!

She wouldn't be in town long. Sassy was on a mission—personal business—and it was delicate. It might take a few weeks or months to do it right, and then she'd be gone again. Back to the Midwest where she belonged. Before the antelope started to migrate, Sassy would be on her way back home, to figure out her future.

Her task, once accomplished, wasn't going to change her life. It was just something to cross off her list. Even her own mama didn't know why she was here; why she insisted on an internship in Wyoming. There was only one other person who knew and he was gone. It was the one thing her daddy asked of her in his last days, besides keeping an eye on her mother.

That he'd been too cowardly to do this errand himself made Sassy very sad. She always saw her father as big and brave, like a fearless knight. The fact that he turned out to be flesh and blood was an unfortunate dose of reality at a time when she was fresh out of heroes. But losing him was hard enough without being angry, so Sassy tried to focus on the good times and not his failings.

Her dad worked hard setting she and her mom up for a financially generous life. Through the years, it was his number crunching that forged the bond, and it was the reason she'd gone into accounting.

"What are you doing?" Sassy would ask at a young age, bounding into her dad's home office.

"Well, I'm taking care of you, baby girl," he'd say.

"Doesn't look like it," the child would pout, and he'd set her on a chair nearby and show her his computer screen.

"Then let me show you," he'd say.

For years, it made little sense, until she became much older. By then, his calculations and his efforts came together for Sassy, like pieces in a puzzle. She began to understand the concept of savings accounts and interest, and investments; accounts payable and accounts receivable. When she was an adolescent, he explained the trust funds he set up for her, and how they would affect her future.

"Now some say that a young person won't work hard if they know they have money waiting for them in the bank," he told her more than once, "but I believe in you, Sassy. You'll work hard no matter what. Right?"

"Right," she agreed with a smile. She'd agree to anything for her beloved father, but on this he was right.

CHAPTER 4

"*T*he prodigal son returns at last!"

"Hah," Ash laughed as he walked into the imposing West Ranch kitchen and hugged Ridge hard. Either his dad had gotten shorter, he noted, or he himself got taller while he was away. "There's a lot of implications with that comment," he said. "It's been a while, but I haven't exactly been running away."

"I know, I know," Ridge conceded, reluctantly loosening his hold on his youngest. "And you've got the diploma to prove it."

"Don't go acting like I haven't seen you in years," Ash said with another good-natured laugh. "Y'all were at my graduation, just weeks ago."

"But this is different," Ridge swallowed the unexpected emotion. "You're home. And that means something."

It meant something to Ash too.

So did having the entire West clan fly to Michigan State University to celebrate his degree in livestock management. The Wyoming Wests sure did make their presence known, hooting and hollering louder than any other group in the stands when he walked across the stage—and Ash didn't mind in the least. On the contrary. He moved his tassel to the other side of his mortarboard, and lifted his diploma in the air with pure joy and triumph.

And maybe a tear or two.

Ash wasn't raised a West, but now, thanks to MSU, was qualified to join the family business with a solid foundation. His honors-level diploma implied that he would be an asset to the ranch. No longer the know-nothing kid who had to fall off a horse a time or two just to learn the ropes, he was proud of his achievements, and glad he changed his mind four years earlier about business school.

"Congratulations on being accepted to Columbia University," the letter read. Boy, how the family had celebrated when that piece of mail arrived! But as summer went on, Ash felt a stronger tug to join his dad and brothers at West Ranch.

Maybe he wanted to belong, or pay his family back for taking him in as a lonely teenager—one who was going down the wrong path. Or maybe he just wanted to work alongside the Wests. Ridge and Gunnar, and Rowdy and Gray, were some of the finest men he'd ever known. Colton and Pike, though no longer working on the ranch, lived just minutes away and were always available to listen and give advice to Ash.

However it happened, West Ranch had gotten under Ash's skin.

He got chills every time he drove through the tall iron archway emblazoned with a massive WR, which stood for his name—the name that chose him. A name he wanted to pass along to his own sons and daughters someday. Unlike him, they would inherit the name at birth, along with full rights and privileges. Ash wanted to earn it and care for it; nurture it, and show his appreciation to the ranch and the name.

If he didn't love these things, how could he expect his children to?

Funny, thinking about children at such a young age. It was not something his friends and roommates had on their mind—far from it. They were thinking about girls, and cars, and signing bonuses for their entry-level jobs. But when a boy is abandoned by his parents, fixing things for the next generation is top of mind.

At least, for Ash it was.

"You're an old soul," one girl at MSU told him, and Ash didn't think it was a compliment. He'd been trying to explain his vision for life on the ranch. A heavy conversation for a sorority party when the others were talking about their lake homes and favorite ski hills. But Ash didn't care. Having clear goals and a vision kept him from making foolish choices that would derail his plans, or dating girls who weren't open to living in Wyoming.

"You watch those Michigan girls, now," Ridge told him as he packed for his freshman year. "They're tempting sirens, each and every one; tall and willowy, with blonde hair that turns to spun gold on the beach."

Ridge was only half joking as he said this—his first wife Randi Lynn, now deceased, hailed from northern Michigan. Her alma mater was the law school at Michigan State.

"I'll watch out," Ash told his dad.

"You do that," Ridge said, "because there aren't many women willing to leave those Great Lakes for plains and hills. Even with this beautiful gorge out our back window, the isolation here can be a tough sell."

That was only the beginning of the advice that came his way. Everyone pulled him aside and chimed in.

"Work hard and remember," Gunnar said, "once you graduate, the ranch work will be harder than you can imagine. But I'll be proud to have another West at the helm."

That one got him, for sure. Thankfully, Colton didn't reduce him to a puddle of tears. "Don't be the last one to leave a party," the middle brother advised. "Always leave alone. *Always.*"

"Yes sir," Ash promised, and kept it.

"Take an art appreciation class, just for kicks," Pike encouraged.

"Enjoy the autumns," Kat suggested. "Don't tell anyone I said this, but Michigan has Wyoming beat when it comes to fall colors... and it doesn't snow there in October."

She sighed wistfully, making Ash hopeful that she'd come and visit him a time or two.

"I hear the gas stations in Michigan sell sushi," Liu warned him.

"Stay away from that. Some of the better grocery stores, now that sushi would be okay. Oh, and ignore Colton's advice. You don't have time for parties. As my parents told me, '*We are not sending you to school to party—good grades, that's your party*.'"

Liu's no-nonsense ways always made him laugh. She also made him a box of spring rolls to eat on the way to the airport. He wouldn't take a car his freshman year; he'd live in the dorms and stay close to the campus. Making Paislee's advice challenging.

"Take a day trip to the Detroit Institute of Arts one Saturday, when the weather is good," she said softly. "Take in the Diego Rivera murals, titled *Detroit Industry*. I guarantee, they will move you, and give you a great appreciation for the concept of work."

Her words were so touching as she spoke to him like an adult—like someone he'd yet to become, but would very much like to be someday. Holding her baby boy, Ford, in her arms, Paislee kissed him on the cheek and added, "Don't forget to come home to us, Uncle Ash."

CHAPTER 5

*H*ome.

Sassy felt a twinge of jealousy when that handsome cowboy said he was going *home*. Home as she knew it would never be the same. Her father was gone, and her mother was distracted by her new independence—financial and otherwise.

The little colonial she grew up in near the Missouri River was small, but in a tidy, desirable neighborhood where massive big-foot homes were replacing the quaint small houses at a rapid pace.

A picket fence defined the front yard, and a rose-covered trellis led to a brick-paved patio in the back. More times than she could count, Sassy joined her parents there for three-handed pinochle and cold lemonade.

Sassy was grateful for the loving home, but didn't see herself returning after graduation. Not permanently, anyway. Her mother was young, and made it clear she wasn't relying on her daughter to help her navigate widowhood.

"I'm going to mourn, Sassy," she had said with a loud sniffle. "But each of us will find our own ways to move on."

One day, before leaving for Wyoming, Sassy came upon her mother's open computer screen to see she'd been taking virtual tours of the town's more modern condos. Beautiful two-bedroom apartments with soaring ceilings and terraces—condos without any roses to prune, or fences in need of fresh paint.

The rooms in the photos looked cold, modern, and void of personality or warmth. She'd like to think her mother would turn any place into an inviting home, but without her father's influence, didn't hold out much hope. He was the sentimental one; the one who picked out their plush furnishings and art. Left to her own devices, her mother would stick a *Moving Sale* sign in the lawn, and sell everything down to the bare walls.

Except for a photo or two, Sassy doubted she'd be able to distinguish her mother's new place from a hotel room.

"This *granny* cottage was your dad's dream, but I think it ages me," she said, making Sassy think the little house would be sold by the end of summer. Maybe it would be for the best—the only thing Mama liked to paint was her nails.

The house was paid off, and the sale would more than cover the price of anything her mother wanted to buy. She felt a stone in her stomach at the realization that her mother wasn't sentimental about the things Sassy held dear. Maybe that was for the best. She'd always see her father in the nooks and crannies of the little home; waiting for her in his office, which had become a walk-in closet for Mama's expanding wardrobe.

"What?" Her mother had been defensive as the daughter flipped through the clothes and gaped at price tags. "Your daddy liked to see me in pretty things. He wouldn't want me looking all dowdy on account of his dying."

Sassy smiled, knowing it was true. And also understanding why he'd set up her mother's inheritance in monthly installments, so she couldn't blow through it all too quickly.

"Just pace yourself, Mom," Sassy had said. "You have more dresses than places to go."

"Hmm," was the non-committal reply she got.

In any case, Sassy made sure to pack up her belongings in stackable storage boxes that were clearly marked, in the event her mother up and moved. She wasn't ready to have her childhood thrown out with the trash.

CHAPTER 6

*H*ome.

  When Ash left four years ago for Michigan, things had been changing like crazy—like a whirling dust devil on the prairie.

He himself was a recent high school graduate.

Dad and Casey just returned from their honeymoon in Italy and Switzerland, and bounced around between the ranch, the town and Casey's house in Phoenix.

Colton and Liu's massive rustic home on the ranch was being built adjacent to the tea house, complete with a guest house and the beginnings of a kitchen garden—all along the scenic West River.

Pike and Paislee welcomed baby Ford, and were waiting to adopt one-year-old Sun, who was taking her first steps. Both children were heirs not only to West Ranch, but were the newest generation in the wealthy banking lineage of their Denver family. Paislee's sister, Poppy Andrews, the new CEO of First State Bank, was already anxious to groom Sun to take her place someday.

Ash's niece Willow, Kat and Gunnar's baby, had been toddling around the ranch four years earlier, adorably saying his name with a silent A. "...*sh*, ...*sh,*" she'd say.

Now, Willow was five and a half, Sun was five, and little Ford was four. Each unaware that they were multi-millionaires; each more interested in catching bugs, riding bikes and splashing in the river. And tumbling into Ash's room, as they did this morning.

"Uncle Ash! Uncle Ash! Get up," they screamed.

"Mama said we could wake you, 'cause it's summer vacation," Willow said.

"Yeah," Ford chimed in, his pudgy hands landing soft blows on Ash's mid-section, "it's summer *bacation*."

"Gettup gettup," Sun said in a sing-song voice, overexcited by the little parade.

"Okay, okay little people," Ash relented, trying to pry his eyes open. "I'm getting up. But *only* if there's coffee. Is there coffee? Who can be the first to find out?"

The children laughed and screamed *"me! me!"* as they ran towards the kitchen.

Is there coffee for Ash?

Ash quickly jumped out of bed to lock his door so he could hop in the shower without the little visitors barging in again. He'd slept late. And in spite of what Ford said, his summer *bacation* was over. He'd already deferred his job at the ranch by three weeks after graduation to enjoy time at his friend's Michigan lake house before driving home.

ERIK OLSEN WAS THE NEWEST IN A LONG LINE OF AUTOMOTIVE engineers in his Detroit-based family. His parents owned a sprawling summer house in the northern lower peninsula, on Lake Charlevoix, with access to Lake Michigan.

The "cottage," as the Olsen's called it, had six bedrooms and five bathrooms—in addition to an outdoor shower for "leaving the beach outside," as Erik's mother liked to say. There was a sleeping porch with bunkbeds, and another directly below for rainy-day reading, and mosquito-free evening meals.

The walls were painted blue, and trim everywhere was bright

white. On the walls, photos of several generations of the Olsen family documented their reunions in front of the house.

Ash was in love—with the house, the family, and with Michigan summers.

Every day, he and Erik would wake early and push the sailboat into the calm waters of the inland lake. Catching a breeze, they'd sail under a drawbridge and wave to people at the many outdoor patios and decks along the channel. Then they'd reach the greatest of the Great Lakes, where they'd clip the waves and fish for bass and perch.

In the heat of the day, they'd drop the anchor and swim to shore for a burger and beer under a shaded outdoor umbrella. One glorious day, they sat on the beach and watched a regatta of sailboats racing to Mackinac Island—an exclusive location nestled between Michigan's upper and lower peninsulas.

Every night, they'd dine on the screened-in porch with the rest of the Olsen clan, then go to various beach parties with long-time friends of Erik. And *yes,* he'd be sure to tell his dad, a few of the girls did have hair that looked like spun gold from the Michigan sunshine!

Three weeks flew by, and before Ash knew it, he was thanking the Olsen family for their hospitality, and extending an invitation for them to visit West Gorge anytime, to see a different kind of beauty.

"We have a full guesthouse on the ranch, and you'd be welcome to it."

Ash described the mountains and the river, and the proximity to the Grand Tetons, the Wind River Mountain range, and Yellowstone National Park.

"I'll come for sure," Erik said, with sincerity. In his board shorts and a faded tee shirt, along with a stripe of zinc oxide sunblock on his nose, Erik was getting ready for a day on the water and Ash felt a pang of sadness that he had to leave. But a big part of him was also anxious to get home.

After his farewells, he turned his loaded pickup truck towards the west and started driving. Saying goodbye to Charlevoix, to Lake Michigan, and to some of the best years he'd ever known.

Caught up in the emotion, he felt the urge to stop in town and pick up a real estate catalog—maybe buy his own cottage on Lake Charlevoix. But common sense prevailed; he'd only be able to visit a week or two every summer. And though he had the money, a half a million dollars was a big impulse buy for a two-bedroom, one bath cottage.

Wasn't it?

CHAPTER 7

*L*eaving Michigan had been hard for Ash, but returning to West Ranch was the right thing to do, he was certain. With his degree, Ash stood tall, ready for his first "real" job. He wasn't the unwanted orphan, tagging along on weekends with whichever of the Wests had time to teach him a thing or two—generous though they were with their time.

"Assistant Manager, with a salary and profit sharing," Gunnar told him at graduation, with a clap on the back. "Same deal me and the other brothers got after graduating."

The other brothers, was a term that played over and over in Ash's head like a ticker tape parade, as he showered and dressed for the ranch. He was one of the "other brothers," and could hardly wait to show up and prove himself. If their enthusiasm at his college graduation was any indication, there would be another celebration upon his arrival and Ash was excited for the acknowledgment and attention.

Instead, he found the parking lot nearly empty of the ATVs and Jeeps used for day-to-day business—*where was everyone?* He was later than usual, sure. He thought everyone would expect it after his long drive. Still, Ash felt deflated walking into the big empty room. His bootsteps echoed off the poured cement floor, and Gunnar and Rowdy's offices were dark.

But with a start, Ash realized the room wasn't as empty as he'd thought.

"There's a dead tree in the creek, up by the gorge," a voice said, coming from a girl behind a desk. Ash didn't see her when he walked in; her face was half hidden by her large computer screen, which held her full attention.

He immediately recognized the yellow waves of her hair.

"You need to go clear it," she continued, still not looking at him. "It's blocking the drinking water for the herd. If you don't know where it is, I'll get you a map."

Ash was stunned—the beautiful Bo Peep was sitting behind the desk of the ranch office!

Because she wasn't looking up, the girl couldn't see his delight and surprise, or the frown that quickly followed. Ash expected to at least find Gunnar and Rowdy in the ranch office to greet him on his first official morning, maybe even Gray. He didn't need a hero's welcome, but a welcome of any kind to his new position would have been nice.

After all, Ash didn't have to come back to West Ranch. He could have stayed in Michigan, or anywhere in the world, for that matter. With his degree, experience, and the West name, he had job offers and ranches vying for his attention.

"You know, there's livestock to manage right here in Michigan," his friend Erik mentioned one day while at the lake. "It would be great to have you nearby."

"Don't think I'm not tempted," Ash said, but knew he'd never not go back to Wyoming when his visit was over.

Now, a dark cloud passed through his fragile heart as he gazed at the nearly empty room—the indoor picnic tables were abandoned, and the food tables were being cleared by the kitchen staff. His brothers were nowhere to be seen and a girl who wouldn't even look at him was barking orders, like he was a day hand.

She obviously didn't know who he was.

"Oh, I know where it is, Bo Peep, but what makes you think I'm going to do that thankless task?" Ash asked, sounding petulant and prickly, even to his own ears.

The girl paused only a moment from clacking on her computer keyboard, then kept working. Her head was down, and she refused to give him the courtesy of a glance, but couldn't completely hide the smile playing on the corner of her mouth.

"Bosses orders. You're the last ranch hand to arrive. Rowdy said latecomer gets the muddy creek. Oh, and he wanted me to tell you work starts at seven, not mid-morning."

Ranch hand! Ash thought. *She doesn't know that I'm the boss. One of them, anyway.*

The girl swiveled in her chair, then stood quickly and walked towards a filing cabinet. She couldn't see Ash's jaw drop as he took her in.

He *knew* better... he knew not to judge a girl by her curves and golden hair. His brothers and sisters-in-law had drilled that into him. And yet, the way she floated with a carefree walk made him forget everything else.

Ash stood still, trying to breathe her in. She smelled like fresh air and wild clover.

"Plenty of hands looking for work this summer," she said, finally turning towards him. "I wouldn't be late again if I were... you. It's *you.*"

The girl froze where she stood and looked mutely at Ash's eyes—when her own eyes glazed over and began to flutter heavily. In a flash, Ash saw her knees buckle just slightly and he knew she was about to fall.

"Whoa," he yelled, lurching forward to close the gap, catching her in his arms. Ash wrapped both hands around her torso and waist and pulled her tight to him, allowing time for her limp body to recover. He could feel her long legs trying to get purchase on the pine floor, but didn't want to let go too soon.

The girl moaned a little and shook her head. Instinctively, she wrapped her arms around his neck like a life support ring, and gripped him tightly. Anyone walking into the office would see their embrace and think they were dancing, or sharing a lover's first kiss—two things Ash silently added to his summer wish list.

"Hey there," he crooned softly. "You okay?" His hands, he realized, were resting on the bare skin on her back, under the soft cotton of her shirt. Quickly forgotten was the anger he'd felt towards his family at not welcoming him today, and the growing impatience at the way this mysterious girl had bossed him around.

But why did she faint?

"Oh... wow..." With effort, she found her strength and began to pull away. "I thought I was over the altitude sickness, but I guess not. Rowdy and Gunnar warned me against making sudden moves."

The girl laughed a little as Ash led her to an office chair, then dashed to the refrigerator to retrieve two bottles of water.

"Sip one, and I'll hold the other on the back of your neck."

She looked up skeptically, but reached behind her head to pull her locks over one shoulder. Dipping her head like a delicate gazelle, she offered her neck to Ash while gazing up with soft suede-brown eyes.

Ash's hand shook as he placed the water bottle on her flawless skin. When she moaned again, Ash thought it might be his turn to lose his footing and fall to the floor.

"Second time you saved me," she said, "I guess I should know your name."

His mouth was dry. When he did speak, he purposely withheld his last name. She followed suit.

"Ash."

"I'm Sassy."

"Hi Sassy," he recovered as she straightened her torso and inhaled deeply.

"Well, I guess the dead tree it is," he fumbled, "if you're okay alone, I'd better be going."

"Want some help? I've been staring at this computer screen too long and could use some fresh air."

She smiled at him, and it was the loveliest thing he'd ever seen—prettier even than a Lake Michigan sunset, or the blue of Lake Charlevoix sparkling like diamonds in the sun. Prettier than the waterfalls in the deep gorge just outside of West Gorge, or the fluttering aspen leaves in September.

"It's going to be a muddy mess, but come along if you want…" Ash managed to say, in a voice that sounded like he was an adolescent again. But Sassy was such a surprise, and he desperately wanted to be next to her, and to talk with her. If only he trusted his own abilities. Could he drive the ATV without crashing into a boulder? Could he operate the chainsaw without cutting off his own limbs?

"Great," Sassy said, standing slowly to gather her sunglasses and work gloves. "Rowdy told me to take breaks from the spreadsheets and tag along here and there, to get to know the operations of the ranch. I've gone on a few outings but the creek is new to me."

So is this feeling. Ash could feel a herd of butterflies stampeding wildly in his stomach.

"As long as I'm spending the summer on a Wyoming ranch," Sassy said, slipping her arm through his, "I might as well learn to be a cowgirl."

CHAPTER 8

"An electrical storm swept through Chicago once, when I was an intern. One minute, the sky was blue and cloudless. The next—it was dark as night. A wind blew down the street by the hospital like it was shot out of a cannon, and shook the building. The street lights were going sideways, like this."

Kat West flattened her hand to show her husband, Gunnar, the position of the lights. They were sitting on the deck of the ranch house eating their lunch, facing the gorge and enjoying the sunshine.

Gunnar took a sip of his iced tea as he listened.

"Needless to say," she went on, "the storm hit hard, complete with sheets of rain, flashes of lightning and crashes of thunder."

"Wow," he said. "That's a lot of weather adjectives."

"Oh yeah, all the adjectives. But then the power went out, which completely overwhelmed the generators. In the doctor's lounge, anyway. We were pretty low priority as far as emergency power went."

"Uh huh," Gunnar stayed with the story, though he had no idea where it was going.

"For five whole minutes, I sat in the dark," Kat said. "I'd been checking my email at a desk in the lounge, so I just waited there. Then the lights came back on, and I put my hands on the keyboard once again... *and then...*"

"And then?"

"Yep," she said theatrically, "a surge of electricity zapped my hands, and the computer started smoking!"

"Holy smokes," Gunnar said, "a power surge? You mean to tell me the hospital didn't have surge protectors on their shared computers?"

"I'm sure they do now," Kat said.

"Wow, now I won't be able to sleep tonight until I check all our surge protectors on the ranch," Gunnar said, shaking his head, "and don't take this wrong, Kat... but how did we get here, conversationally speaking? Weren't we talking about the summer ranch hands Rowdy and I hired?"

"Were we?"

"Yes," he said, "there's the three fellas from Dirk Trainor's old ranch, they know what they're doing."

"Uh huh," Kat nodded.

"And there's Freda Lang, plus Wayne, Red and Jackie's nephew," Gunnar continued.

"Wayne's all grown up. He's been working at Red's BBQ empire, but wants to see what the big deal is with ranching, right?"

"That's right," Gunnar said. "And then there's Sassy."

They were silent for several seconds.

"Ah yes, Sassy."

Kat sounded like she tasted something bad. *"That's* how we got here, conversationally. When I met her at the ranch office and shook her hand, I felt that same electrical power surge as the one in Chicago."

"Well, she is from the Midwest, come to think of it."

"There's something about her I don't like, Gunnar."

"She's smart. Always on time or early," he said, "and that's good. She's helping us wrangle some of the financial loose ends of ranch business."

"Okay."

"Sassy doesn't mind hard work or getting her hands dirty, even though she's..."

"She's what?" Kat knew the answer, but wanted to hear Gunnar say it.

Her husband seemed to choke on his words, and Kat secretly enjoyed watching him squirm a little.

"Well, she's awfully... she *looks*... she doesn't look like a typical ranch hand, I guess."

"She's gorgeous," Kat offered, and Gunnar shrugged in agreement.

"Sassy isn't the first woman we've hired on the ranch, but she's the most..."

Gunnar stumbled again.

Curvy? Smoking hot? Beautiful? Kat wondered what he was trying not to say.

"Qualified," he said at last. "She recently graduated with a degree in business and accounting, with a minor in livestock management, same as Ash."

"Ash!" Kat exclaimed. "That's another thing. What kind of influence will she have on Ash, young and vulnerable as he is?"

Gunnar laughed a low rumble and took Kat's hand.

"Sassy is young and vulnerable, too. Besides, mama bear, it's not for us to control."

"Maybe he won't notice her," Kat said, hopefully.

Just then, they turned to the sound of an ATV roaring across the sagebrush, between the ranch house and the gorge. The ATV was heading towards the creek.

The loud laughter of two people trying to be heard above the engine traveled up the cliff to where Kat and Gunnar could hear. The driver was tall, with dark hair. The passenger held one hand on her cowboy hat, with golden blond tresses flying around her face.

It was Ash and Sassy, no doubt.

"I think that four-wheel-drive has sailed," Gunnar said.

CHAPTER 9

*W*est Ranch hadn't been looking for summer office help. Rowdy made that clear to Sassy in their first email exchange, back in the spring. But she was persistent. To his credit, Rowdy emailed her back every time.

"Send your resume and we'll keep it on file," he told her.

Like a dog with a bone, she sent Rowdy a note every few days, hoping to wear him down. "I need work experience more than money. Maybe you would consider a low-paid internship," she countered. "I can help manage the office, and shadow the hands when possible. I have a fancy new degree and zero ranch experience."

"Here at West Ranch, we believe men and women should be paid fairly for their work, so I can't agree to those terms," Rowdy replied.

"Another reason to join the team. Your work ethic is refreshing," Sassy countered, trying a little flattery.

"Other ranches might be hiring, I can put in a good word," he'd offered.

"But West Ranch is the biggest and the best, and I'd rather not settle."

At last, Rowdy relented and offered her a summer position in the office. "We do have a few loose ends that need tying up. Our on-site bookkeeper left suddenly for a family emergency. I've been picking up the slack, but numbers aren't my strong suit—forgive the pun. Perhaps you can help us out, and I can get back on the range."

"That sounds perfect," Sassy told Rowdy with great relief. She'd been trying to keep the desperation from her tone, not wanting to tell him, or anybody, her real reason for coming to West Ranch.

Not yet.

Rowdy wouldn't let her anywhere near the ranch if he knew, she was sure. Now that she was here, she told herself to just be cool, and lay low until the time was right. And for goodness sakes, push any thoughts of that young, handsome Ash into the background.

He's not making it easy, Sassy thought to herself as he drove the ATV towards the creek.

Every time she was in a little bit of trouble, there he was. Like earlier, when she got up too quickly to walk to the filing cabinets. Sassy figured the worst of the dizziness was past, until she found herself in the very capable arms of the new summer ranch hand.

"This high mountain altitude takes some getting used to," he said.

Rowdy cautioned Sassy about the same thing a few weeks earlier, when she wondered aloud why she felt glued to her swivel chair.

"My legs feel so heavy, like I can't stand," she half laughed, half whined to Rowdy. Instantly, she was sorry to have mentioned any of her body parts—Sassy liked to stay under the radar as much as possible. Her "natural beauty," as her mama called it, was like a bright lantern she tried to keep doused.

"Takes a while. Drink a lot of water," Rowdy advised.

Ash was also the one who rescued her the day before, when she was stranded. And all Sassy knew about him was his first name.

Gunnar and Rowdy weren't any help. Earlier that morning, they simply said one more ranch hand was expected. "We'll find some thankless job for him, as a welcome," Gunnar told Rowdy, and the two smiled wicked grins.

What she did know what that he was a lot better looking standing in front of her desk than he appeared on the deserted road. And even more handsome—devastating, really—holding her after catching her.

With his arms around her waist, she got the full affect; the kindness and concern in his eyes, the highlights in his dark hair, the dimple that appeared in his cheek when he moved the muscles in his jaw, and even the scent of his morning shower.

He smelled good. But everyone on the ranch did first thing in the morning. Once he started hauling the felled tree from the creek, with the hot sun beating down, that good smell would be gone in no time.

Smiling, Sassy thought back to the day before, when she sat on the trunk of her car and tried not to laugh as Ash *shepherded* the sheep off the road, so a tow truck could reach her.

"Shoo! Shoo!" he called, trying to gently prod their hind quarters with his makeshift staff from a fallen tree limb.

Maaa maaa, they called back in protest, digging their hooves into the asphalt and gravel.

"Come on boys, work with me here. The pretty lady has to get to town, and I have to get home." He sounded so sincere when he spoke, Sassy found herself rooting for him.

Surprisingly, the sheep responded to his heartfelt plea, and so did she. It wasn't the first time a man had called her *pretty*, far from it. But it sounded different coming from the mouth of this very young man— it was pure and sweet, as if he'd never said *"pretty lady"* before in his life.

The way the boy spoke the words sounded just a little bit sacred to Sassy, and something near her heart squeezed tightly.

Once he had the road cleared, Tig's Tow truck came over the hill. He greeted the driver as an old friend, and gestured to Sassy, who had put clothes on over her bikini. Then he tipped his hat to her and got in his truck to wait and follow. And he was gone.

Until this morning.

CHAPTER 10

"Are you sure you know where the creek is?"

Sassy turned to talk to Ash as he guided the ATV across West land. She held one hand on the top of her cowgirl hat, while the other held tight to the ATV's grab bar to steady her on the bumpy ride.

"It's my first day, but not my first summer at West Ranch," Ash disclosed, still elusive about who he was. He smiled over at Sassy as she grinned in happiness, at the beautiful sunny day, no doubt. He wanted to keep his identity from her as long as possible so she could form her own opinions of him, separate from the West family.

Sitting so close to Sassy, Ash felt the weight of his name—a name he was still growing into. Sure, he joined the Wests at community events, and took part in board meetings for the foundation. He weighed in on decisions that would affect the family and the growth of the ranch—buy this property or that; donate which acres to the town; where to develop?

But today he understood for the first time the ramifications of being an owner of the ranch—the ranch that happened to hire the prettiest girl in the world as a summer intern.

If he asked her on a date, even just to the movies, lots of people in his life were going to have opinions, and his family's objections would be merited. If she went out with him, other ranch hands could claim favoritism. If she declined his invitation, she could claim harassment.

It was a minefield in a sea of sagebrush.

For the first time, he appreciated the dilemma Colton was in a few years earlier when the beautiful Liu Chen came to work as a chef for the family. Kat didn't want Colton kissing the cook, she told him. And wanted to protect the family name and reputation.

"Liu Chen could do a lot of damage if she doesn't share your feelings," she'd told Colton. "Especially if she feels pressured to date you."

Love won out, though, and the two were married the summer before Ash graduated and left for Michigan. But Liu was a Wyoming girl, through and through. Whereas Sassy was destined to go back home in the fall.

One big reason to keep a respectable distance.

WHEN THEY REACHED THE FALLEN TREE AT THE CREEK, ASH TRIED TO help Sassy with the thick tree trunks and spikey, scratchy branches. But she just laughed him off.

"Such a *gentleman*, offering to do my job for me," she teased, using her best impression of Scarlett O'Hara. "Thank you, Rhett Butler, but I have to make my own way in the world."

"Well Miss Scarlett," Ash bantered back as the swarthy Clark Gable, "I'm just trying to get us back to Atlanta before it's all burned down." He was glad he stayed awake during the four-hour film for one of his extra credit classes, instead of just reading the synopsis.

Sassy laughed even harder, and the time flew as they talked about their favorite movies, winter sports, and food.

"*Gone With the Wind* was epic, but it was no *Tombstone*," Ash declared.

"I declare, that's blasphemy," Sassy stated in her best southern belle voice.

"Hmm, best change the subject," Ash said. "Skiing or snowboarding?"

"Snowboarding is overrated, and downhill skiing is going to make a splendid comeback," Sassy was sure.

They debated the pros and cons of Chicago-style pizza versus Detroit style.

"Detroit style, hands down," Ash said, and to his surprise, Sassy agreed.

"I can't fall on my sword for Chicago style, I'm afraid," she said. "Not when Detroit makes the crispiest, cheesiest crust."

"At last," Ash said theatrically, "common ground."

He was beginning to feel more relaxed in her company, when Sassy suddenly dropped a tree limb she had been tugging at and let out an ear-piercing wail.

"*Ahhhh.*"

Throwing off his safety glasses and gloves, Ash rushed to her side, splashing through the creek as he went.

Sassy had sat down hard on the creek bank, and held one hand in her other. Ash sat down next to her, the side of his body fully against hers.

"Ow ow ow," she cried out.

"Here, let me look." Ash gently but firmly took her hand. As she turned away, she let out another cry. "Oh, that's a bad splinter," he said, "it went right through the glove."

"I... *know...*" she wailed louder.

As Ash worked her glove off, Sassy's cries turned to resigned sobs. Shaking, she held her hand as still as she could, allowing Ash to tend to her. She had her eyes squeezed shut, and opened them only when she felt Ash setting a small branch upon her lap.

"Here, bite down on this stick, Scarlett."

His face was close and his words were whispers she could feel on the bridge of her nose.

"Did you say bite... *down?*"

Ash nodded somberly.

"We're going to have to amputate."

In spite of her pain and fear, Ash heard Sassy expel a surprised laugh at his joke. When she did, he pulled out the offending splinter in one swift move, before she could protest.

She turned to him in shock and wonder as he hung onto her trembling hand.

"You were so brave, Scarlett," Ash laughed softly. Without warning, he pulled her hand to his lips and kissed—*tasted,* really—her finger. As he warmly wrapping his lips around her slender digit, her gasp was so spontaneous and unpracticed that Ash felt his chest tighten with unfamiliar joy. He gazed over and ventured a look into her eyes.

"All better?" Ash's voice was low and scratchy.

"All better," she said back, in a whisper that would haunt his attempts at falling asleep for many nights. Seeing her eyes widen, and her lips parting ever so slightly would play over and over in his memory like a closed loop.

He knew he shouldn't have done any of that.

"Do you know how many germs are in your mouth," his Granny would demand to know when he was a boy, trying to cleanse a scratch with a little spit.

But there it was, her small hand resting in his. And then there were all those tears, and his longing for… something. Before he knew it, he had her perfect porcelain finger between his lips, savoring it like a candy cane and watching her eyes for a reaction.

So much for keeping the beautiful girl at a distance.

CHAPTER 11

"*S*urprise!"

Ash and Sassy jumped a mile when they walked back into the ranch office to a roomful of people and boisterous hoots and hollers.

With boots wet from the creek, muddy jeans, and scratches on their shirts from tugging on the rogue branches of the downed tree, the two were bedraggled and exhausted pulling into the parking lot, but laughing together about many things.

Ash had been grateful for Sassy's help as they'd used the chainsaw, then removed thick lengths of the tree's trunk with the ATV and a rope. It was a few hours of grueling labor, but the water now flowed freely again for the herd's drinking water.

"You did great, cowgirl," he told her. "Job number one is looking after the cattle, making sure they have food and water at all times. Unless there's a dry spell or a downed tree, nature provides the water just fine to those that graze along the river. For the others, we have an intricate solar-powered system of pipes and troughs."

He was rambling, he knew, knowing his cover would likely be blown when they got back to the offices. Sassy looked over and smiled indulgently as he talked. She was probably exhausted, especially since she'd nearly passed out earlier from the high altitude of the mountains the ranch was nestled in.

"I swear, I forgot what hard work was like until today. This ranch has a way of reminding you how pathetic your book knowledge is compared to your arms and legs." Walking into the office, he was about to comment that day one of cowgirl school had been a success, when they were accosted by a celebration of sorts.

"Wha…" Ash looked around the room to see all the ranch hands looking back at him expectantly, along with Gunnar, Colton, Pike, Rowdy and Gray, and even Ridge. Gunnar stepped forward and patted Ash on the back, gesturing to a food table filled with burritos, tacos, canned pop in iced buckets, and a large cake.

Congrats Grad, the cake said.

"Here's to the newest ranch manager, Ash West," Gunnar said proudly to the room, and then to Ash. "Welcome to the team."

Sassy moved quietly behind Ash and slipped off to the side. Genuinely surprised, Ash smiled and gave a little wave to the room.

"Wow, thanks," he said, truly touched.

Everyone hooted and clapped as Ash turned red with pride and embarrassment. As the hollering quieted down, Ash figured it was time to say a few words. The food was getting cold and if everyone had a morning like he did, they were hungry.

"Thank you, Gunnar. You know how to make a fellow feel special, saving that old muddy tree for me to pull out of the creek—well, that was just about welcome enough," Ash said good naturedly to general laughter. "Can we eat now?" That's when the room really exploded. Ash went off to wash the mud off his hands and face while the hard-working hands ate heartily in his honor.

"Well done, son," Ridge spoke quietly as he clapped him on the back. The two men tossed their paper plates loaded with food onto the table and sat down to eat.

Ash thought he knew what his dad meant.

BBQ and cake were the equivalents of big-city inter-office memos that heralded a promotion. Men and women on the ranch who were twice and three times Ash's age needed to be aware of the family's intentions, and know enough to place "the kid" in higher regard. The tree in the mud—well that was Ash's opportunity to show he wasn't too high and mighty to tackle even the most menial of jobs.

Always be willing to do what you ask of others. He'd been shown time and again.

"Just two small tacos, Dad?" Ash gestured to Ridge's plate.

"Oh, Casey's got me tracking my fat, carbs and dairy. She and her henchman, Doctor Kat, are on me to change my ways."

Ash smiled. "I'm glad to hear it. Just because you've got three grandchildren…"

"A fourth on the way, with Liu and Colton's baby," Ridge pointed out.

"Right, four grands," Ash said, "doesn't mean you're still not a dad. And I suspect I'm going to need you more than ever this summer."

"So I see," Ridge mumbled, looking across the room at where Sassy sat, eating and talking to Freda Lang and Wayne. Even with her hair pulled back and a smear of mud on her face, the girl was drop dead lovely.

Ash would have to be blind not to notice her.

CHAPTER 12

"Turns out, that so-called ranch hand that came in late for work today is Ash *West!*"

Sitting with Freda in the living room of their rental house, Sassy ate her bowl of chili, holding the spoon stiffly with her bandaged hand. The boy who couldn't seem to stop rescuing her was an heir to the West fortune, and he couldn't take his eyes off her.

This last thing wasn't new to Sassy. Her young life was dotted with looks and leers from men, along with jealous glances and a few daggers from women. She was her beautiful mother's daughter, something her mother reminded her of all the time. But where the mother *invited* the looks, the daughter wanted no part of them.

"Yep, he is," Freda answered distractedly in between hearty bites, with one eye on a muted television show.

When Rowdy finally hired Sassy, he offered her a shared "bunkhouse" with Freda Lang, another summer hire who lived in Lander, a few hours away. This was Freda's third summer on the ranch, Rowdy told her.

"You'll like Freda. Everybody does," he said.

Sassy agreed to the terms and braced herself for rustic lodging.

Instead, the bunkhouse was an adorable bungalow in town with a common space and modern kitchen, along with two bedrooms.

Rowdy was right about Freda, and the girls became fast friends. Freda and Sassy took turns with the cooking—Sassy making summer salads and vegetable casseroles, with fresh fruit for dessert. Freda, in contrast, cooked sloppy joes, mac and cheese, and her favorite, chili.

"Prince Ash, I call him," Freda said with a giggle.

"Oh?" Sassy was intrigued. "Why is that?"

Freda put her bowl in her lap and smiled at Sassy.

"Well, it's like this," she drawled. "West Ranch is a bit like a kingdom—the most powerful in the land. Ridge used to be the king, but he handed his crown to Gunnar. That makes Kat West the queen. Not just of the ranch, but of the town, the family... of everything she surveys."

Freda used a free hand for a grand sweeping gesture to punctuate her last words.

Sassy got a chill up her spine at the insight into the West family, and gave Freda her full attention.

"Tell me more."

Freda went on to give Sassy a history lesson about Wyoming ranches.

"Time was," she said, "ranches were small mom and pop organizations, and every building did double duty. The main house was used as an extension of the ranch—for meals and gatherings. The ranch wives were in the thick of things, cooking for hands in the busy season and such. They kept the books and ran errands—they'd go back and forth to town for machine parts and supplies, in their spare time."

"Not much of *that*, I'm sure," Sassy said, and Freda nodded in agreement.

"Plus, they raised the kids and did all the laundry," Freda added, "kept a garden and preserved food for winter... tended their own live-stock... volunteered at church."

"You say West Ranch is different?"

"Now it is," Freda said. "Today, West Ranch is more like a large corporation. Or like I said before, a kingdom. And queen Kat has the luxury of keeping all the messy, dusty, dirty ranch work separate from her castle. I don't blame her; I'd do the same."

Sassy murmured in agreement.

The once-modest ranch had an expanding infrastructure of outbuildings, cook houses, bunk houses, feed storage, barns, sheds, equipment garages and so forth. The hands gathered each morning in a large building that housed offices, lockers, picnic tables, showers and bunk beds.

There was a kitchen, next to a long counter for serving food. Most days, the hands were welcomed by breakfast burritos or sausage scrambles. The ranch cooks also put out a hearty lunch or early dinner, depending on the day's scheduled tasks. There was always fresh coffee in the stainless dispenser and maybe a cookie or two on a tray.

Sassy, who manned the reception desk outside the offices occupied by Gunnar and Rowdy, was intrigued by the picture of West Ranch Freda was painting.

"And where does prince… I mean, Ash, fit in?"

"Prince Ash will for sure take over one day when Gunnar and Rowdy are ready to retire," Freda said, scraping the bottom of her bowl for the last chili bean. "The other brothers aren't involved anymore, so Ash is next in line. It's a big responsibility, with an equally big payday."

"And…" Sassy spoke gingerly, being careful to appear dis-interested, "there's no princess for the prince… that you know of?"

"Not unless there's someone back in Michigan. The way he looks, though, it's only a matter of time. That will be one lucky girl, but she'll have to be tough enough to dethrone the queen. I have a feeling Kat won't give up her position without a fight."

"Interesting," Sassy said quietly.

She knew Ash was interested in her, but again, it was nothing new.

"Lots of men will think they want you," her father told her many times before he died, "but you get to decide what and who you want. Don't ever settle."

Did she want Ash West? It was too soon to tell. He was funny, kind, and very good looking. And while his wealth didn't interest her, he did have something she wanted: access to the front door of the ranch, and the heart of the family.

Maybe, Sassy thought, maybe she'd been handed a gift.

CHAPTER 13

*H**er skin was like silk!*
Staring at his ceiling and struggling to fall asleep, Ash grabbed a handful of his soft sheet, trying to recall the sensation of having his hand on the small of Sassy's back earlier when he caught her—the intrusion wasn't intentional, but the feel of her tormented him nonetheless.

His head was swimming at the memories of their encounters and in his half sleep, he dreamt of holding her and dancing with her; being near enough to catch her any time she stumbled—over anything.

How quickly she'd gone from being a stranger to the pretty girl he'd rescued, touched, and holy cow, even *tasted* before the day was through. A big grin broke out on Ash's face as he remembered.

SASSY'S PRESENCE DULLED THE SURPRISING PAIN ASH HAD BEEN FEELING as he mourned the end of his university years. He never wanted to go so far away to school, yet Ridge had pushed him hard.

"Most teenagers can't wait to leave the confines of home to cut loose a little," Ridge told him. "And I understand why you're reticent to leave home, Ash, but it will be here when you get back. So will I."

Ash choked up at his words. Just the reminder that he had a home and a dad got him every time.

"Go find yourself, son. Explore the world and trust your safety net," Ridge implored, with full understanding, Ash thought, of how hard it would be to leave the family he'd been gifted after his world fell apart.

"We'll be here whenever you come back, and you'd *better* come back," Ridge added.

At first sight, Michigan seemed a foreign land. Flat, for the most part, without any of the mountains and valleys that Wyoming had in spades. But he quickly learned to love its unique beauty—Michigan had trees for miles. Ash had never seen so many trees, or such vivid fall colors.

Kat was right.

Winters were amazing. There was none of the hunkering down that Wyoming ranchers had to do. In Michigan, winters were celebrated with skiing, snowboarding, ice hockey, and sledding down the nearby golf course hills on borrowed trays from the college cafeteria in the wee hours of the night.

And water! So much water, everywhere he turned. Someone told him that you only had to drive fifteen minutes in Michigan to reach a lake, river or stream.

While Wyoming waters never seemed to warm—even the smallest lake was newly melted snow from the mountain caps—in Michigan, lakes the size of oceans welcomed swimmers and boaters for months.

The Great Lakes blew him away.

By the end of four years, Michigan had gotten under his skin. Ash felt a sadness at leaving the crystal-clear water and beaches, and his friends. But Sassy reminded him of the youth and energy of his Michigan State University days—indeed, she grew up in the next state over from MSU, and her voice flowed in the same cadence as the Midwest girls in all his classes.

None of this *y'all*, or the *aw shucks* folksy speak he was made fun of for during his first year. Sassy sounded buttoned up and crisp, like a honey gold apple in a Michigan orchard.

"Sassy!" Still wide awake, Ash spoke her name to the ceiling.

Usually he had no trouble falling into a dead sleep after ranching or renovating. A good day's work was the best remedy for insomnia Ash ever knew. But tonight, his thoughts were swimming in a beautiful sea of Sassy. Every time he was about to nod off, his heart raced at the memory of her golden dewy skin, bright smile, and hair the color of chilled curls of fresh-churned butter. Not every girl could wear sunshine in her hair the way Sassy did.

"It cannot be," he scolded himself, pushing thoughts of her away. "Michigan is my past. There's only Wyoming, now and forever."

CHAPTER 14

The sun was rising the following morning as Sassy and Freda got to the ranch offices. In spite of the early hour, ranch hands were already there, drinking coffee and talking about the day ahead. Among them were Ash and the other West men.

Freda walked over to the breakfast table, while Sassy dropped her purse on her desk and booted up the computer.

"Good morning, *Mister West*," she said pointedly to Ash.

"Guilty," Ash said sheepishly.

Sassy smiled and continued her greetings. "Good morning, Mister West, and Mister West... and Mister West."

Ash, Gunnar, Rowdy and Gray all laughed good naturedly.

"You know we're on a first-name basis, Sassy," Rowdy said. "It's too early in the morning to be pickin' at us; wait until we've had more coffee."

"Okay fine," she smiled. "I'm not *pickin'*, it's just that a certain somebody forgot to mention his last name when we met. But I think it's great that your family is still so involved and invested in West Ranch, after what, 140-some years?"

"We've had a few strays jump the fence," Gunnar chimed in, talking, no doubt, about Colton and Pike, who went off to other ventures.

Colton was one of the busiest developers in West Gorge, and Pike was an artist, with a growing number of galleries anxious to sell his original landscapes.

Ridge, the current patriarch of the family, had more or less retired; his interest wandering after losing his first wife, Randi Lynn. Upon marrying Casey a few years back, he fully handed the reigns to Gunnar so he could "enjoy his honeymoon." Apparently, it was still going strong, four years later.

"Well now, don't forget a few others came along to take up the slack," Gray said. "I guess that's the upside of having a large family—like Freda, here. The Lang clan easily rivals the Wests in number. Right Freda?"

Freda nodded, having wandered over with her coffee and a breakfast burrito to join the conversation. The ease of which Sassy envied.

"How about you, Sassy," Rowdy asked. "Do you have a big family?"

Sassy smiled before answering, not wanting to sour the easy banter in the room.

"Nope, just me and Mom," she said, "since Daddy passed."

The men collectively frowned and shook their heads in sympathy.

"Naw, it's okay," Sassy assured them. "Daddy was a stock broker. A job that doesn't take a small army, the way West Ranch does."

Her tone and comment managed to lighten the mood again, and everyone moved away to refill their mugs and grab a bite to eat. Everyone that is, except Ash. He stayed near her desk, his dark eyes shadowed in concern.

"How long ago did your daddy pass?"

His tone was quiet and confidential, which touched Sassy.

"Nine months ago," she answered. "Beginning of my last year in college."

"That's gotta hurt."

Sassy shrugged, but gave his comment a nod. It was clear by the way Ash planted himself next to her desk that he wasn't going anywhere until he got an authentic answer from her. It was, she thought, an unusual display of empathy for a man so young.

"It hurts worse than a splinter from a fallen log in a creek," she said at last, looking up. Then, with a slight smile, added, "it's probably not a boo boo that can be kissed away by a handsome cowboy."

Ash's eyes remained compassionate, Sassy noted, until the corner of his mouth pulled up in a partial grin as he arched one gorgeous eyebrow.

"Maybe that depends on the cowboy, ma'am."

He bowed his head slightly and touched the brim of his hat before turning to walk away, leaving Sassy a bit speechless, and a bit stirred at the thought.

CHAPTER 15

*S*o, Ash West wanted to try his hand at flirting, did he?

Sassy sat at her desk. She was flushed, in spite of his novice attempt. And more than a little amused. Watching Ash flirt was like watching a newborn calf struggling to walk on uncertain, spindly legs.

Freda didn't mention the flirty side of him, she thought. But perhaps Ash hadn't flirted with Freda. Though Freda was a pretty girl, and easy to get along with.

Yet with Sassy, Ash was all "depends on who's doing the kissing."

Flirting for Ash was probably very new—like a boy trying on his daddy's ten-gallon hat; checking the mirror to see how it fit. She wanted to tell him that it didn't fit him.

Not at all.

He was too nice, and too genuine to be pretending to be someone he wasn't. Then again, his attempts were so endearing, and she didn't want to deflate him.

She also wanted to tell him that she'd been flirted with by the very best, her entire lifetime. Men and boys—mostly single—had been falling over themselves to get her attention since she could remember, and she always found it off-putting.

"Someday, you'll like the attention," her mother told her, but that wasn't true. Not yet. She might make an exception for Ash West, who probably had no idea how handsome he'd become since his high school days, according to Freda. Or how attractive it was when he was just being himself, like stopping to help her with a flat tire, only to end up herding sheep. Or catching her as she fainted. A man who would gently hold a water bottle on a lady's neck was someone special.

But it was the splinter that did things to her legs, and stomach, and head when she thought back on it.

The way he told her he had to amputate just to make her laugh, and the way he supposedly kissed her finger—*kissed it,* like her finger was sleeping beauty and he had to prove his love, was, to date, the most swoony kiss Sassy ever received in her young life. And it was only her little finger.

Imagine if and when that kiss landed where it was supposed to.

But flirtation was something to be avoided—it's not why she came to West Ranch. Sassy was here for a very specific mission that had very little to do with Ash West.

Or maybe it did.

Maybe flirting with Ash wouldn't be so terrible. There might be hurts a man like Ash could kiss away, if she gave him the chance. And just maybe he could be a shortcut to her ultimate destination—the big house on West Ranch.

CHAPTER 16

"*Y*ou're not putting on the sun block I bought you."

Sassy stretched her long, tired legs out in front of her on the sofa and looked over at Freda, who was tucked into an oversized chair. Fresh from the shower, they both sat in shorts and tee shirts, watching the sun set out the window of the bungalow.

It was Friday night, and they were both starving and exhausted—almost too tired to lift their tacos and glasses of milk.

Freda, Sassy noted, had a bright red nose and cheeks. She wasn't as tall or as lean as Sassy, but seemed happy and comfortable in her own tawny skin. Sassy admired her sense of humor, and easy way with all the "fellers" on the ranch. Sassy knew that she herself came off as aloof to some, but learned to be overly cautious with boys and men, lest they think she was flirting with them.

"Mixed messages," is what some accused her of relaying, when she refused, politely, a date. Almost always, she had just been acting *friendly*—just like Freda did so naturally.

Better to be thought a snob, she decided at a young age, than a flirt.

"I know, I know," Freda shook her head. "I was just trying to get a little sunshine; a little tan, before I go home tomorrow. Why don't you come with me? We'll get James Timothy Freemont to take us both to dinner."

"Jim Tim is going to take one look at you, and think *you* are dinner; a lobster dinner from New England," Sassy said, causing Freda to laugh at the nickname she'd given her boyfriend. That Freda never stopped to realize this possible name herself confirmed to Sassy that the girl was definitely in love.

"Jim...," Freda had to pause and laugh again, "Jim Tim is going to *owe* me a lobster dinner after not answering his phone this week, or returning my calls." At that, the girl's smile faded just a bit, and Sassy felt her pain.

"Freda, that boy is studying to take his law school finals," Sassy said with all the positive energy she could muster, "so he can be a big shot lawyer in Lander, Wyoming, and build you a ranch, where your eighteen babies can run and play, and herd cattle when they're four."

Freda's face broke into a smile again.

"Where have you been all my life, Sassy?" She said, and then added, "I'd like that life with Jim Tim. Come to think of it, maybe I'd better not take you home to Lander. He'll take one look at you and..."

"*Stop.* That's not how it will ever be, so don't say that."

Freda looked sheepish.

"Sorry Sassy, you can't help how you look."

"Sure I can," Sassy broke into a wicked grin. "I can skip the sunblock, just like you do."

"All right all right," Freda laughed. "Touché."

To Sassy's ears, her friends word sounded like a long drawl, like "too *shayyy*," and she joined the laughter. It was easy to be with Freda. She wanted to be her friend and visit Lander, just like any normal girl. She wanted to see what the Lang family was like—did they bicker over the hot water in the shower, or the last donut in the box? Sassy hoped so. As an only child, she longed to experience the lovely loving chaos of larger families. She wanted some drama, and laughter.

And Sassy fervently hoped that Jim Tim would barely notice her, same with Freda's father or brothers. She merely wanted to be Freda's new, anonymous, forgettable friend.

Good old *what's her name.*

"I'm sorry, what?" Sassy realized Freda had been talking.

"I was saying that I used to think Ash West was cute, but he never paid me any notice these past few years—but he sure does look good this summer."

"Well I've never seen him before this summer, so I can't weigh in."

"Then I'll weigh in for the both of us," Freda said. "He looks *good.* All grown up, and ready for something, and someone."

"Tell me more about Ash," Sassy said casually. "But first, promise me and mean it this time, to use that sunblock. Or else your pretty tan is going to turn into a complexion akin to that antique leather saddle the Wests keep in the ranch office. The one that used to belong to some dead guy named Pickford."

"*Akin.* Jim Tim. You just crack me up, Sassy pants," Freda snorted, then sat back to tell her new friend everything she knew about the West family, and Ash.

CHAPTER 17

"*D*on't forget to stop in and see Amber in town."

Casey stood in the kitchen of the ranch holding a cup of coffee. It was Saturday, and Ash was up early to enjoy his first day off since returning home. The ranch still demanded attention, but Rowdy and Gunnar had hired a weekend crew to spell the regulars, and rotated managers to oversee the workload.

"Her storefront, Amber Waves, is very popular with locals and tourists," Casey continued. "It's just down from the mercantile. Amber asks about you all the time."

Ash only had a few friends in West Gorge, and one or two seemed mighty close to retirement age. But he planned on going to the town, to say a howdy or two.

Kat sat at the table flipping through magazines with Paislee, and Casey joined them. The three liked talking about decorating trends, among other things, as Kat was continually improving the ranch house, and Casey had her houses in West Gorge as well as her Phoenix house.

"Stop by the Arts and Culture Center," Paislee said. "Pike has new paintings on exhibit."

Ash nodded.

"Where's Willow, Sun and Ford?" He couldn't help but notice how quiet the kitchen was without the exuberant voices of his little nieces and nephew.

Kat smiled. "Saturday mornings, the kids all go to Auntie Liu's house for Chinese cooking lessons and language school. She started teaching little Sun, but Ford and Willow did not want to be left out."

"Of course, Liu's baby is due in a few months," Casey said. "She might want to slow down a little."

Then after a pause for affect, everyone in the kitchen broke into a laugh at the thought of the energetic Liu ever slowing down. The chef took the ranch by storm when she arrived five years before, and maintained her demanding job even after marrying Colton West. It wasn't until their new home on the West River was completed that Liu helped Kat hire her replacement.

These days, Liu worked her kitchen garden, created videos for her food blog, and looked after her husband and extended Chen family—now permanently installed in the guest house adjacent to her own sprawling home, eagerly awaiting the birth of Liu's first baby.

Liu still brought over large platters of food to the ranch house, prepared by herself and the Chen women, "for our family." Every morsel was appreciated and devoured by Kat, Gunnar, Willow, and whoever else happened to be under the roof at the time. Often Ridge and Casey, and now Ash.

In warm weather, Liu served garden-to-table dinners in the cool shade of her custom tea house; a gift from Colton. Hers was an idyllic life, according to the million-plus fans following her videos and social media posts.

Before Ash left for town, Casey stood up from the table and gently took his arm. She pulled him close and kissed his cheek.

"It's so good to have you back, Ash," Casey said. "We've all missed you."

Ash smiled and returned the affection. Since marrying Ridge, Casey had doubled down on her friendship and maternal gestures. Having no children or siblings of her own, Casey gladly traded any reticence she had about joining such a close family for an openness that was without guile or agenda. She just wanted to be with the man who made her heart skip a beat, and would navigate any other relationship that stood between them.

Turned out, everyone wanted to be her friend—eventually.

Casey wasn't going to challenge queen bee Kat to be the head of the extended family—she didn't want that role. She wasn't going to take on Liu's cooking dominance, or try to one-up Paislee's sense of style and design. She wasn't going to tell anyone how to raise their children or love their spouses. Casey was learning these things for the first time herself.

Early on, Casey decided to allow the West sons the time they needed to accept her in the family; to smile and be an extra hand when one was needed, and then practically run to whatever bed Ridge West was laying his head on any given night, and fall into his arms.

Four years before, he had saved her life, in more ways than one. They had been inseparable ever since.

Liu Chen's mother, Ling, once told her that according to a Chinese proverb, if somebody saves your life, they are responsible for the rest of your days. But later confessed that she and her husband, Zhang, may have gotten their wisdom from David Carradine in a *Kung Fu* episode rerun.

"Either way," Ling said with a smile and a shrug, "Ridge West is a catch."

CHAPTER 18

"Casey girl, you're looking mighty good today," Ridge said to his wife later that morning, as she passed him in the ranch suite where they often stayed.

"You said the same thing last night," she answered with a breathy laugh. Casey enjoyed staying at the ranch, but found herself talking in whispers, as if in a museum. When in fact they were completely isolated from the rest of the family.

"It was true last night, and it's true now."

Ridge reached out for her hand and pulled her to him. Wrapping his arms around her waist, he sunk his face into the warmth of her neck and kissed the lines of her jaw as she worked her arms up and down the muscles of his arms and shoulders. She seemed to enjoy his strength, he noted, like other women enjoyed ice cream, or fancy coffee drinks. Probably because she'd been on her own for so many years. Casey drew courage from her husband, breathing him in with great appreciation.

He made sure that every day she knew beyond a doubt that he would be strong for her, and that he cherished her. Ridge was making up for lost time. He couldn't imagine a beautiful woman such as Casey having to wait until practically fifty years old to know the love of a good man. It was boastful to think of himself as such, he knew, but in comparison to the lowlife who crushed her heart and her business back in Phoenix, he was an undisputed saint.

So he wooed her and courted her. Flirted with her. He sent fresh flowers to her office and fancy boxes of chocolate-covered cherries. In the night, Ridge kissed the place on her neck that made her inhale sharply and reach for him, and caressed her arms and neck in the dark until she fell soundly asleep.

This was no "rocking chairs-on-the-porch" sunset marriage—Ridge West was working harder and more *intentionally* than he ever had. After being the man who rescued Casey from a blizzard and a pack of ravenous wolves, he refused to live by halves. In other words, the way he'd been carrying on since the death of Randi Lynn.

As a result, he could swear Casey West looked younger and more youthful each day as cares were stripped away from her heavy heart. Secretly, it was Ridge's new benchmark for success. Putting that vulture, Casey's ex, behind bars, had been a guilty pleasure.

The scumbag wouldn't stay locked up forever. Just long enough to mark him guilty for his embezzlement, and for the local newspaper to absolve Casey of the pain she felt at leaving her father's real estate business in ruins. As a result, she was more at ease returning to Phoenix and visiting her childhood home—which had been thoughtfully renovated into a retreat for the two of them.

The guilty verdict also triggered a restraining order, following the dude's attempts at blackmail.

All in all, their first years of marriage didn't have the same highlights as other newlyweds, but both Ridge and Casey came with a bit of baggage, which they both eagerly signed on to help each other carry. Now, they could put the more unpleasant things behind them and just enjoy each other's company.

"It's great having Ash home," Casey said as they sat with their mid-morning coffee in their private rooms.

While they were in Europe after their wedding, Kat had the suite completely updated with plush carpet, sage green walls, and decadent crown moldings. She hung new paintings, and brought in swivel club chairs with a shared ottoman so the couple to enjoy the view of the gorge. Thanks to a polished walnut butler's pantry, they could make their own coffee and toast in the morning when they wanted to linger.

"He's looking good," Ridge agreed. "Says he might move into his bungalow for the summer, though. I don't know how I feel about that."

Casey shrugged.

"He's finding his way," she said. "He's not a kid anymore, or a student. Certainly his neighbors in town are easier on the eyes than his family."

Ash's bungalow, which he inherited from his grandmother, sat next to the Parks Place rental that Freda and Sassy were living in for the summer. Ridge grumbled once he connected those dots.

"More reason for Ash *not* to move there."

"Oh, why's that?"

"I like that Sassy," he said carefully, "she's just… too pretty. That could be trouble."

Casey frowned at the comment, but didn't have to say anything.

"Oh, I know how bad that sounded, and I'm sorry," Ridge said. "I just sense she's going back home after the summer, and I hate to see Ash get hurt. But I can't protect him from pain—he's a grown man now."

CHAPTER 19

$\mathcal{A}$ sh had granny's bungalow rented out for most of his university days, thanks to Casey and her property management team. Just recently, the little family who had been living there gave notice and moved up to Idaho.

"Should I advertise it for you?" Casey wanted to know, and Ash declined.

"I might live there myself for a time," he'd said. Now, he was glad. For upon pulling into the driveway this Saturday morning, Ash saw a beautiful girl with yellow hair walking from the mailbox at the next house over. It was Sassy, he knew, and she was distracted, carrying a mug of coffee and wearing a short little sundress.

"Morning, Bo peep," he said, getting out of his Jeep.

She looked up, startled.

"What are you doing over there, don't you live at the ranch?" She asked.

"This is my granny's house. Well, used to be hers," he said, "she left it to me. I renovated it, same time that Casey renovated the house you and Freda are in. Same time that my dad renovated the house on the other side."

"Wow, what a little fixer-upper party that must have been," she said with a smile.

Ash nodded.

"It wasn't dull, that's for sure." He was thinking about the antics of Ridge and Casey as they fell in love with each other.

"Is your house the same as ours?" Sassy pointed to the rental she and Freda shared.

"Not exactly. Of course, I haven't been in mine for some time. Renters have been living here while I was off at school."

"You must be anxious to take a look around."

Oddly, Ash wasn't. He'd stand and talk to Sassy all morning, if she'd give him the time.

"I'm a little nervous and reluctant, tell you the truth. It used to be my home when I was a boy. More and more, it's becoming just a house."

"Well come in and have a cup of coffee with me first," Sassy said with a sweet smile. "I always think it best to put off uncomfortable moments. And I have Saturday bagels."

"Cream cheese?"

"Of course," Sassy said. "A true Midwest delicacy. I'd get bagels every day of the week if I could, but Freda and I never have enough time to swing by the Donut Den before work—we're always running nearly late. So Saturday it is."

"All right then," he said, walking towards Casey's little Parks Place rental. Sassy turned and led him into the house, her exposed skin shining with coconut butter. Ash tried to pry his gaze from her long legs so he could look around the house. "I remember when there was sawdust everywhere, and doors that needed to be hung."

"Doors are hung, thankfully."

"Freda must be sleeping behind one of them," Ash said, wandering into the kitchen.

"Nope, she went to Lander again to see her guy. Sit down, I'll bring you a plate."

Ash did this gladly, as he found himself shaking a little. She just smelled so much like the girls at the beach in Michigan, and looked like them too. Ridge said to be careful of the Midwest girls, but here was one—right in Wyoming. Sassy was the most beautiful girl he'd ever seen. But she was nice, and the other day at the creek, they'd laughed and talked like old friends.

Now that she knew he was a West, he wondered if she'd treat him differently. And now that he was an owner of the ranch and she an employee, he *knew* he needed to act differently—didn't he?

"How's... how's your hand?" Ash wanted to quickly get off the subject of being alone in Sassy's house with her. Just the thought seemed to stir up rumblings in his stomach that he couldn't account for.

"My hand? Oh, the splinter." she said, handing him a plate with a warm bagel from the toaster. "Well, Doc West, it healed right up. Either from the extraction or the kiss. I haven't decided yet."

She was so pretty, and the memory of wrapping his lips around her porcelain finger as they sat by the creek, with her wide eyes looking at him in surprise, would have buckled his knees if he wasn't sitting.

Ash exhaled a puff of air, realizing he'd picked the wrong topic if his goal was to avoid the provocative.

"So, your father..." he attempted, lamely.

Sassy cut him off, laughing at his obvious discomfort.

"Ash West," she said, taking a bite of her bagel and lifting her coffee mug as she appraised him. "I suspect we'll have lots of time this summer to talk about sad things such as my father and your grandmother. But it's a perfect day, so let's not spoil it."

Relieved, he smiled and ate his breakfast.

"Since my car is still being repaired," she said, "why don't you show me around West Gorge today. I haven't seen much besides the ranch and the grocery store. And something called the *Mercantile*, where they sell cast iron pots and fishing poles, and thick shirts that feel like they're made of old tarps."

"Yep, that's about it," Ash laughed.

"I did buy these boots, though." Sassy lifted a tanned leg to show Ash the expensive leather-tooled Mercovas that graced her feet. His eyes traveled from the boots to her shin, to the cap of her knee, and then along the toned muscle of her thigh, stretching up and under the hem of her short, but casual morning dress.

"Wow, pretty," Ash said, thinking, *pretty pricey for an intern.* He tried to keep his eyes on the boots, and not the glow of her flawless skin. "Have you been to the West Gorge Arts and Culture Center? Or up to Cindy's Diner?" Ash's voice sounded scratchy, like an adolescent.

"No, but I'd like to see more of West Gorge, and Wyoming."

"Okay, let's do it. How about I tidy up your kitchen while you go get dressed."

Sassy wore a mischievous smile on her face as she stood. He was mesmerized, and couldn't look away.

"Done," she whispered.

Spinning around like a dancer to walk down the hallway, Sassy moved her hands to the hem of her sundress, then lifted her arms in one swift motion over her head—taking the dress with her. Barely breathing, he watched, spellbound, as she turned into her room wearing only her pink bikini.

CHAPTER 20

"*I* wish I was normal."

At a young age, Sassy began to understand that she was beautiful. Not just pretty, like the Katies at her school, or interesting, like the Lindsay's. She had the kind of beauty that made both men and women trip over their words as they stared at her—mesmerized. Like she was an alien or something.

She came home from school one day and complained to her parents, telling them how much she wished she could blend in.

Her mother just laughed, delighted.

"Of course you're not normal," she crooned. "Look at the two of us."

Indeed, her mother was gorgeous. And her father looked like a movie star from long ago, before leading men could look like her gangly string bean science teacher, or the moody boy that bagged their groceries with a long swoop of hair hanging in his face.

Sassy herself was like a cocktail the two had created at the peak of their perfection and ingenuity. Even her name was one of a kind— which didn't really matter in the grand scheme of things. She'd be just as pretty if they'd named her Shlumpy or Frumpy, she knew.

She tried to minimize herself in her adolescent years, slouching her shoulders and hiding her face. Until her father made it his mission to discourage these efforts.

"Would you believe it," he told her once, "that teenaged years are difficult for everyone, no matter what you look like?"

She didn't believe it.

"But it's true," he insisted. "You're all going to get through it, and I'm right here with you." Then he coached her, and encouraged her to take charge of her life, and not allow her beauty to define her.

"Your loveliness is an *aside*," he said. "It's incidental. You are smart, and you will design your life according to your own vision, not anybody else's. You won't let any man control your beauty for his own selfishness—you will decide what and who you want. Not the other way around."

He spent years staying close and guiding Sassy. He told her how to be above reproach in conversations, and how to avoid gossip and innuendo. He insisted she only go on group dates, and suggested other ways to avoid being vulnerable.

"Don't ever be in a position to rely on the *kindness of strangers*," he said, after they'd watched a very old movie with the famous line. And she hadn't—not until her car ran into a rock to avoid running into a herd of sheep. Then she relied on the kindness of Ash West. If he hadn't been so disarming, she would have locked herself in her car, with her index finger poised on a can of spray mace.

As her father's life came to a close, he told her other things, too. Weighty things. Before she left for the university, he told her the secret he nearly took to his grave.

The thing that brought her to Wyoming, and West Ranch.

It was also the reason she was openly flirting for the first time in her life. Surprisingly, it was a little bit of fun, especially with Ash West. He got the ball rolling by kissing her finger once he removed the splinter—and it was no innocent peck. It was a kiss that made her face turn two shades of red, and made her toss and turn at night.

Sassy flipped her hair over and brushed the sleep out of it, then chose a celery green sundress from the closet. She could hear Ash placing the last of the dishes in the drainer as she rolled on lip balm—her only makeup, ever—and grabbed her sandals and sunglasses.

"Be right out," she called to Ash as she finished getting ready for their day; the *date* that she engineered out of the blue after seeing him drive up next door. At the very least it would get her out of the house for the day.

At best, it would get her one step closer towards accomplishing her task.

CHAPTER 21

*T*heir tour began with a visit to the Amber Waves store in town, where Ash's old pal Amber looked glad to see him, but not so glad to see the beautiful Sassy trailing behind him.

Her greeting went from "*Hey* Ash!" to a tepid "oh hi," when introduced. As for her part, Sassy was warm and friendly, browsing the store enthusiastically while the two old *pals* caught up a bit. Amber had stayed in town after high school, first attending a community college, then an online business school. Between her internet sales and assisting Casey with her real estate management, Amber was doing quite well for herself.

"Look how tall you got, Ash," Amber exclaimed, looking up at the boy, who merely shrugged. He thought she sounded a bit sad, but didn't know why. There was definitely distance between them now so he couldn't ask her so freely—he'd barely seen her in the past few years, when he tended to spend his holiday time in Michigan.

"I s'pose."

He looked around the storefront and shook his head in wonder. She had expanded into the vacant store adjacent to her, and also expanded her product line from vintage finds to Wyoming souvenirs and reproduction antiques. Half her store looked like it came out of a magazine, with rustic home goods strung with fairy lights.

Faux dining tables were set with antler-handled coffee mugs, stamped burlap runners, and plates designed with black bears marching around the rim.

"What a beautiful store," Sassy said as she rejoined the two. "I'll have to come back before I leave town and buy my mama a gift."

Amber visibly brightened at the comment.

"Oh, you're not staying in West Gorge? Pity."

"It is a pity, isn't it," Sassy replied, "I only have a summer internship at West Ranch. Of course, if someone were to offer me a job I might stick around. Maybe you'll have an opening in the fall, Amber."

Amber fidgeted a little, before shaking her head and answering.

"I hear the Pet N' Feed store is hiring a night time cage cleaner," she said at last.

Sassy held onto her smile while her eyes narrowed at Amber— almost imperceptibly.

As Ash watched, the girls reminded him of two bighorn sheep squaring off to do battle.

"WELL, WELL, ASH WEST. YOU'RE A SIGHT FOR SORE EYES!"

Sassy hung back in the hospital gift shop, amongst the *Get Well Soon* pillows and cards, while Ash got an enthusiastic hug from Marta Scott, the manager.

"To think I knew you back when you were a teenage *pickpocket*," Marta blurted loudly to a blushing Ash. He smiled big, though. Sassy was glad to see he could take a little ribbing, and couldn't wait to hear the rest of *that* story.

After introducing Marta to Sassy, they made polite conversation for a few minutes—Marta asking Sassy all kinds of too-personal questions. Where was she from, who was she dating, and did she plan on staying in Wyoming. Sassy managed to be polite but evasive, then slipped away to pretend to read the greeting cards.

Marta raised her eyebrows suggestively at Ash and whispered

theatrically, "and here I was gonna put your love life on the West Gorge prayer chain. I see God already dropped a perfect angel right in your lap."

Ash cleared his throat uncomfortably at the image. Sassy was suppressing a smile, he could tell, as he glanced her way across the small store.

"It's not like that, Marta," he choked out. "But I'm knee deep in ranch work and my new job, so my love life doesn't need intercession at the moment." Ash knew the power of West Gorge prayers and could only imagine what trouble the church-going people in town could stir up for him. Why, they'd have him dating, engaged, and married by the Harvest Fest.

A bun in the oven by Christmas.

"Don't forget to stop by the jail and say hi to my son, Jason," Marta said as the two prepared to leave. "He's captain of the police force now, but you'll always be his favorite lockup."

Sheesh.

Ash knew he'd better go before Marta said any more. As it was, Sassy was getting a very in-depth look at his past. Maybe he should drive her past the school where he played hooky as an adolescent; or to the local grocery store where he stole canned goods to feed his Granny—that would complete the picture.

Getting back in his truck, Sassy was blessedly silent, but she was watching him closely.

CHAPTER 22

"*D*on't mind my asking," Sassy said from the booth later at Cindy's Diner, "but why do cowboys dress like... well, *cowboys* on their days off?"

"What do you mean?" Ash set his cheeseburger on the plate and looked down at his jeans, boots, and pearl-snapped plaid shirt. Suddenly, he knew exactly what she meant.

"When you were at school in Michigan, what did you wear on warm days?"

Ash thought about his carefree summer days with Erik Olsen, at the beach and on the boat. At first, he borrowed his friend's board shorts and then bought his own. They didn't have mercantile stores along the coast in Michigan—they had outfitters of a different kind. Stores that sold shirts with built-in SPF for long days in the sun, and mirrored sunglasses that cut the glare from the water. There were brimmed sun hats, river sandals and deck shoes. And endless tee shirts with pictures of paddle boards, kayaks and sailboats.

Since he'd been back, Ash had automatically donned his plaids and long jeans, even on days like today. Here Sassy was dressed like a Michigan girl in her sundress, while his summer clothes went unpacked, in a box at the ranch.

"Duly noted," he smiled a wicked grin and picked up a French fry. "But... are you undressing my ranch duds with your eyes, Sassy?"

She let out a surprised laugh.

"No, Ash. I don't have that much time... you're probably wearing long johns under those clothes, too."

It was Ash's turn to laugh. He liked the easy banter between he and Sassy.

"Maybe we should swing by the ranch so you can change before you take me to the gorge. Otherwise you'll be too hot," she said, watching for a reaction.

She had hoped to maneuver their outing into a visit to the elusive West ranch house, whose doors she was keen on going through. But Sassy was surprised at how much she was enjoying her time with Ash, to the point of nearly forgetting her mission.

She found him to be both devilishly handsome and endearingly cute—especially when talking to the prayer chain lady, and the diner waitresses who knew him by name and brought a slice of chocolate cake with two forks.

By the look on his face, Ash didn't remember talking about visiting the gorge and indeed they hadn't. But Sassy needed to get inside the family home.

"Unless," she teased, "today's sightseeing tour of the hospital, the jail, and your old girlfriend are the very best highlights of the area. Here I assumed it was the gorge, waterfalls and the wildlife. Maybe the town should update the brochures."

A dark cloud passed over Ash's gorgeous face.

"I guess I dragged you along on my homecoming tour, instead of showing you things you'd like to see," Ash said as his shoulders dropped. "Sorry about that."

Sassy smiled and shrugged, then took a sip of her milkshake.

"For the record," Ash said, "Amber was never my girlfriend."

"Does Amber know that?"

"I thought so," Ash said, sincerely. "I've barely spoken with her since high school—barely at all in the past few years."

"Did you kiss her in high school?"

Ash blushed deeply, giving Sassy her answer. But he surprised her with his next words.

"What makes you think I'd kiss and tell?"

"You don't need to say a thing, Ash. Your face says it all."

"Dang," he said, looking down at his own milkshake to hide his expression. "I reckon you're getting a big picture of me and my life here in West Gorge, yet I still don't know anything about you. Except you're pretty and funny, and not afraid of hard work."

Now it was Sassy's turn to smile and blush.

"Well maybe you'll learn a little more about me on our trip to the gorge."

"Yeah, we could do that," Ash said.

"After you change." Sassy smiled at how easy that had been. Ash truly was her passport to the West family residence.

"But I think we'll go to the gorge another day when we're both dressed for hiking," he said to her surprise, "It gets cool up in the mountains, and you've got an itty-bitty dress on. Besides, there's one more stop on this tour."

In spite of her disappointment, Sassy couldn't help but laugh. "Let me guess—the drugstore where you used to snitch gum, or a tree where you once carved your initials…"

"…with a stolen knife, of course," Ash grinned.

"Of course."

CHAPTER 23

There was an ease to Sassy that made Ash want to be around her—she was the first woman who made him want to act his age. Ridge was always pushing him to enjoy his youth more while he could, but he never understood the appeal, until now.

She wasn't high school silly, she was more carefree, with an easy laugh. He could make himself smile thinking about her splinter, and the look on her face when he told her he had to amputate. He was never one to tease a girl in any way, but it just came naturally when he was with Sassy.

He also liked how her demeanor towards him didn't change after she found out that he was a West, and a manager of the ranch where she worked. Sassy neither pulled away nor moved closer. She merely stayed as friendly as she was at the creek, pulling dead branches out of the muddy water alongside him.

After lunch, Ash drove to the Arts and Culture Center in town, where he offered Sassy his hand as she got out of the Jeep.

"Just in case the altitude makes you dizzy," he said, gently pulling her soft hand and leading her to an exhibit in the back. Here, each painting had been professionally restored, cleaned and framed, and hung along a curved wall with spotlights. As the two entered the wing, the lights were dimmed to preserve the delicate, ancient paintings, and it was dark and cool. *Romantic,* almost.

Sassy must have thought so too as she squeezed his hand and moved closer.

Breathing in, Ash smelled new carpet and the wood beams overhead. The architecture of the center was designed to evoke the old west and wide-open spaces of the Wyoming plains. There were alcoves with rustic benches and leather chairs for viewing and contemplating—and Ash and Sassy were completely alone.

"These paintings were done in the 1800s by Pickford West—the founder of the ranch and the town, along with his wife, Addie." Ash leaned towards Sassy and whispered. He didn't know why, but wanted to show reverence to his West patriarch and namesake. It was also a chance to place his hand on the small of her back, and gently pull her closer.

It didn't hurt that her hair smelled like lemons and vanilla, and every chance to be near her was a delight to his senses.

Sassy's mouth formed a silent "oh" as she gazed in true admiration at the works.

They moved slowly along the gallery of paintings depicting long horn steers, covered wagons and girls in gingham bonnets. Ash kept his hand on Sassy's waist to guide her, and she didn't pull away when he gently moved his hand up and down.

When they stopped, she was very close—practically nestled against him, putting the entire side of his body on high alert.

"This girl in the bonnet, that's the great aunt of my sister-in-law, Paislee. She came to town with a very old painting, trying to find some information on the artist, *P. West.* She had no idea until she met my brother Pike that he had the other piece of the puzzle—these drawings and paintings that Pickford, *P. West,* did of her ancestor while on the trail. He had them tucked away in the attic of the family's homestead barn. That's how she and Pike met and fell in love."

"You're kidding," she said. "That's amazing. What a heritage you have, Ash."

She nuzzled closer and he looked down in wonder. They'd been touching and standing side-by-side since they entered the center, and it had felt so natural. Sassy's eyes were so wide and beautiful as she gazed up at him in the cool, dark room, that he found his head dipping down as he leaned in closer.

He was planning on whispering to her that it wasn't really his heritage, but what came out of his mouth was completely different.

"You smell so pretty, like a summer day," he said. She started to say something in return, but seemed to change her mind. Instead, she lifted her head and tilted towards him.

Did her lips taste like summer? Ash decided he wanted to find out. He swallowed hard, and her lips parted slightly as a small ribbon of air escaped her, and landed on his neck. Sending a shiver down to his toes.

He bent his head closer until he could almost feel her lips touching his.

"Ash! Sassy!"

A sharp voice pushed them apart, followed by a rustling of noises.

The voice belonged to Rowdy, of all people, who was tumbling out of an office off the gallery with a laughing woman close behind. It was Daisy Shire, Paislee's assistant curator at the art center. In awkward surprise, the foursome stopped and stared at each other.

"Rowdy," Ash nodded, remembering his manners before the others. "Daisy, have you met Sassy... er, sorry, I still don't know your last name, from the ranch?"

"Just Sassy," the younger girl said, nodding to a blushing Daisy, who reached out and shook the girl's hand.

"How do," Daisy said. "We were just... Rowdy was just helping me with..."

"With art?" Ash suggested with a half-smile and an audible exhale of frustration, knowing how close he'd been to a much-anticipated kiss; also knowing that whatever spell he and Sassy had been under at the gallery was definitely broken.

"Art," Rowdy said as if a lightbulb went off, "exactly."

Sassy remained near Ash as the four squared off, and when she reached her hand up to his, he took it easily and confidently. If Rowdy and Daisy could be doing *art* behind closed doors, he could certainly hold a girl's hand out in public.

CHAPTER 24

*R*owdy West came to visit his Wyoming cousins five years earlier, along with his brother Gray, and the two never left. In his early forties, Rowdy had been a long-time rancher in Montana, helping his family run their cattle empire. He also spent time on the rodeo circuit, and had the trophies, prize money and permanent limp to show for it.

When he and Gray came to Wyoming for his uncle Ridge's birthday bash, they were the last two remaining members of the Montana Wests, and at loose ends. They had flush bank accounts from the sale of their ranch, and nothing to tie them down.

Gray was a pilot who spent several months every year extinguishing wildfires in the mountains. But Rowdy had a restlessness he couldn't identify until he came to West Gorge, and saw how stressed and overworked his cousin Gunnar had become under the weight of his sole responsibilities. Ridge was still grieving the loss of Randi Lynn. Pike was pulling away, longing to leave the ranch and follow his passion for painting. Even Colton had his sights set on a different life than the ranch offered.

So Rowdy jumped on an ATV with Gunnar and offered to come alongside him for a time. He and Gray moved into the West's guest house and made themselves at home—Gray coming and going as needed. But Rowdy didn't want to be a guest forever.

After a few years, Casey came into the family with a wealth of knowledge about the real estate market in West Gorge. One day, out of the blue, she asked Rowdy to meet her at a foreclosed log home in West Gorge, just outside of the ranch.

"I wondered if you might like to hang your hat in your own home again, Rowdy," she told him. "This house made me think of you."

He smiled when he walked in and smelled the oak and pine, and saw the soaring vaulted ceiling in the great room. It was a smaller version of the West family home in Montana, but large enough for a growing family, if Rowdy were to have one someday.

The open kitchen had a long granite island, and half a dozen or more stools facing copper-trimmed appliances. A field stone fireplace, flanked by mountain-view windows, would be the perfect location for snowy nights and Sunday mornings.

Outside, there were fenced-in pens for horses, and a pole barn to house Rowdy's ATVs and four-wheel drive cars. Even enough room for his little red sports car that liked to come out and play in warm weather.

There were guest rooms enough so Gray to stay with him when he was in town.

"It's perfect," he told Casey and hugged her. "I'll take it."

Everyone in the family celebrated his official move to Wyoming. Kat West helped him shop for the perfect leather chairs, oversized sofas, and fancy linen bedding and down-filled quilts. Liu stocked his freezer with meals. Colton sent one of his crews out to frame and build a massive deck overlooking the mountains, complete with an outdoor fireplace. Pike gave him an original oil painting of the gorge.

But the best gift began with a simple phone call.

"Now that you're settled, I'm sending a friend over to help with the finishing touches."

It was Paislee West calling him out of the blue.

"Finishing touches?" He was curious. "What is this house missing?"

Paislee laughed at his question, but didn't answer directly.

"Just be home Saturday morning, Rowdy," she said, "and keep an open mind."

More than a little bit nervous, Rowdy showered and shaved early, and was jittery from drinking twice the coffee he usually downed. When the doorbell rang, he jumped a mile and spilled creamer on the floor.

"Coming..." he shouted, throwing a paper towel on the oak planks.

Open mind. Open mind, he said to himself.

The beautiful woman standing on his threshold had a laptop case in one hand, and held the other out to him.

"Daisy Shire," she said, and smiled.

"Rowdy... West."

There was a long pause as Rowdy tried to assess her reason for being at his house—he thought he recognized her from the grand opening of the Arts and Culture Center, but couldn't be sure.

"Mind if I come in?" Daisy asked, grinning with private amusement.

Rowdy followed her to the great room, rubbing his leg self-consciously. His limp always became more pronounced under duress. And the caffeine wasn't helping.

"Ah, this is a beautiful room," Daisy said as she looked up and around. Rowdy watched her face light up at the high windows and lighting. "Paislee was right."

Nodding, Rowdy tried to keep up but felt lost.

"I'm sorry," he said at last, perching on a stool by the massive granite counter. "What was Paislee right about?"

At the helpless tone of his voice, Daisy's face softened as she turned towards him. Setting her computer on the counter, she walked over to the coffee pot and poured herself a cup.

"Mind?" She asked, taking a sip.

Rowdy was speechless. *Was she trying to sell him curtains? A time-share in Florida?*

"Paislee thought it was time for you to add a few paintings to your house, to finish off your spaces. Maybe a bronze sculpture or two. I came to show you a few artists that Painted Bird Gallery represents, and see if anything appeals to you."

You. You appeal to me, Rowdy thought, relaxing at her words and calming tone. A woman who looked right at home pouring coffee in his house—a woman who regarded his eyes and not his injured leg—was someone who could stay as long as she wanted to.

Daisy was about his age or a little younger, he thought. Her hair was a pretty sandy color, and fell in loose waves over her shoulder. She wore snug jeans that showed off her toned legs, and a white blouse with soft ruffles near her neck and wrists. When she was sipping her coffee, he dared a glance at her hand but saw no wedding ring.

Impossible, he thought, with cautious optimism.

Daisy was a romantic, Rowdy guessed by her ruffles and dangling earrings. He liked that. He supposed anyone dealing in fine art must be a romantic by nature. Rowdy himself had a romantic streak, though most people didn't it see under the rough denim and leather his ranching life required.

But he was a sucker for a few frills and a little bit of lace on a woman; throw in some untamed curls, and Rowdy was on high alert.

He found himself smiling at her beauty and easy ways, and gestured to her computer.

"Let's take a look," he said, recovering from his earlier nervousness. "Let's just see what this house is missing."

CHAPTER 25

$\mathcal{A}$s it happened, what the house had been missing was Daisy Shire herself.

After they hung the first painting over his giant fireplace, they sat for a few hours on his sofa and gazed at it together—making sure to catch the landscape in differing lights as the sun traveled over the log house. Daisy brought a bottle of Chardonnay to celebrate, and Rowdy happened to have a charcuterie board in his refrigerator, compliments of Liu.

Hours later, they declared the acquisition a success, and moved on to the north facing walls of the room.

"A trio of seasons," Daisy suggested. "There's a new collection by an emerging painter up in Jasper, Alberta, I want you to see."

Rowdy agreed, and weeks later they celebrated with dinner and a leisurely drive into the mountains.

By the time they got around to discussing the south-facing wall, Rowdy had driven Daisy to her house after a date, where, on her doorstep on a star-filled Wyoming night, he took off his cowboy hat and gently leaned in to kiss her on the cheek. When she smiled at him, and placed her soft hand on his face, he felt the courage to touch her lips with his own, holding the kiss for as long as he dared.

Since that first kiss, Rowdy West began wooing the beautiful art lover in creative ways. In addition to the flowers he sent to her gallery, he attended online art auctions to find unusual pieces he thought Daisy might enjoy. The first time he sent her an 18th century portrait miniature, she was blown away.

"Do you know how collectible these are?" She sputtered in shock.

"I found out," Rowdy laughed. "I made a few enemies in the art world trying to win this tiny painting."

"It's beautiful—I've never owned anything like it," she said. "Thank you."

"Thank you, Daisy, for bringing such beauty into my life," Rowdy gushed with a crooked and bashful grin. "*And* for the paintings."

Daisy soon discovered that Rowdy was much more than the sum of his outward parts. He wasn't just a rough and tumble rancher, but an appreciator of the subtle beauty found in art, nature, and in her. He listened for hours as she talked about paintings and lighting, and finding the perfect frame. And how the right matte could be the difference between a painting feeling "constricted," and coming to life.

Rowdy felt as though he was coming to life under her attention. She saw past the limp; the rodeo injury had been a hit to his confidence, making him shy away from dating.

"When I took the tumble years ago and landed in the hospital, someone who I thought was special, left me," he confided. "She got tired of driving me to physical therapy, and waiting for me to walk again."

Daisy nearly cried when she heard this, and it broke her heart that Rowdy had curled up inside for fear of rejection. He was a wonderful giving and loving man who drank her in like he was parched for her company.

His limp was incidental to her, like the endearing silvery strands in his jet-black hair. Rowdy's beard was also highlighted with the same salt and pepper, and as she spent time with him, she found herself longing to feel his face against her own, and wondered what that would be like.

As it happened, it was soft and heavenly.

It took him forever to have the nerve to kiss her, and she didn't want to let him go when he did. Daisy had already decided that if he opened his heart to her, she would never grow tired of him, or run faster than he could—he could always catch her.

He could trust her.

Before long, Rowdy was popping in to see Daisy at her gallery, or at the art center where she assisted Paislee West in curating exhibits and paintings. Often, he'd ask if she was free for lunch. Sometimes he only had a few minutes for a quick kiss and to make plans for their next date.

Lately, though, she found herself reluctant to leave his log house. And while his eyes begged her to stay, she wanted to hold out for his words. Rowdy was a man of his word, she knew. And she'd waited a long time to hear the right combination that would make her stay forever.

In the meantime, she dared to shake off some of the long dormant dreams of her youth, where they had been gathering dust in dark corners. Dreams of walking to the altar in a white lace dress, where a rugged cowboy would sweep her up in his arms. Rowdy's kryptonite was delicate lace, she realized happily, and pulled out some of her long-forgotten blouses from the back of her closet for their dates—or for everyday office hours, when he might drop in.

When he saw her, his eyes came alive, and she'd reach up to touch the fine crinkles around his tanned and handsome face.

I love you, Rowdy West, Daisy said in her private thoughts, barely able to contain the growing realization.

CHAPTER 26

"*I* pushed too hard," Sassy said in the dark, confiding her closest thoughts to her bedroom ceiling. "With absolutely nothing to show for it."

Except *that...*

She smiled at the memory of Ash putting his arm around her and pulling her close, nearly kissing her in the gallery. Sassy wanted him to. He was so close she could feel his warm breath, and her lips were more than a little anxious and electrified, anticipating his mouth softly connecting with hers. But Rowdy and that woman, Daisy, came tumbling out of the hallway office like a couple of frisky puppies and ruined the moment.

Would there be another?

"Focus, girl," she said before rolling over and closing her eyes. She was getting too caught up in Ash, and forgetting everything else—like, the one reason she came to West Gorge in the first place.

"Dern antelopes."

Freda drove them to work on Monday, slowing down for the

wildlife who were prancing happily without regard to the ranch road or oncoming cars.

In the passenger seat, Sassy was distracted. She could spot the ranch house in the morning light as Freda turned away from it, towards the business offices. Sassy almost got inside, but Ash said maybe next time—when they were dressed for hiking.

Of course there would be a next time. Ash nearly kissed her by the paintings.

Thinking back, Sassy was confused. The day she found out who he was, she decided she'd kiss him if it would get her closer to the house and the family. She wasn't proud of that, but Ash could be a means to an end.

Now, things were getting complicated and confusing.

Now, the *kiss* had become the goal; it was front and center in her thoughts. Nothing else seemed to matter. Even that other thing. When he held her hand in the dark art gallery, and bent his tall frame towards her just a bit, she found herself anticipating Ash West's kiss with her entire being.

Not just because it was part of her agenda.

Oops.

"You didn't hear a word I said."

Sassy turned her head as they pulled into the parking lot. Freda had been talking, and Sassy could not remember a single word.

"I'm so sorry, Freda," Sassy said, reaching over to give her a little pat on the leg. "I've got a bad case of the Mondays, I guess."

Freda smiled.

"I'm not mad, Sassy," she said. "I know where you live. I'll tell you all about my weekend with Jim Tim tonight over beans and franks, and thick slices of fresh tomatoes."

"I want to hear every word," Sassy assured her, getting out of the car. Her own car would be ready to pick up in another day or two, Tig had called to say.

"You did hear every word," Freda replied with a bright white smile that Sassy could see in the early dawn, "you just weren't listening."

Walking into the large wood-paneled room with the concrete

floor, Sassy and Freda saw a few cowboys filling plates with scrambled eggs, bacon and biscuits, as the camp cook brought out an industrial sized pot of aromatic, fresh-brewed coffee.

A subdued chorus of "mornings" made the rounds as Sassy pulled back her desk chair to find a white paper bag. In it sat a fresh bagel from Donut Den, and a small container of cream cheese.

To start your day right, a note on the bag said.

Sassy felt her cheeks get warm as she smiled and walked the treat over to the toaster.

"Bagel? Nobody in Wyoming eats bagels," one of the cowboys teased. "This is biscuit country."

"Oh, believe me I know," Sassy teased back.

CHAPTER 27

"*H*eifer?"

Sassy looked up in surprise at Ash who was standing by her desk. She was just about to take a bite of her cream-cheese-slathered treat.

"No, just a healthy Midwest girl eating a late breakfast," Sassy said before biting down. Most of the crew left for their assignments, and she was enjoying a few minutes of peace and quiet before tackling the spreadsheets Rowdy asked her to create. She thought she was alone, except for the kitchen staff.

Ash smiled in good humor at her response.

"Um, *first,* I would never even dream of... and second, there's a heifer up by the pass who has been late to calve—wondered if you'd like to ride up there with me and check her out. It's a long ride, and I'd like the company. Besides, all good cowgirls need to be familiar with heifers and their calves."

Sassy smiled as she narrowed her gaze at Ash.

"What makes you think I plan on being a *good* cowgirl?"

She could see his mouth fall open as a deep blush turned Ash's neck red.

After clearing his throat and finding his voice again, Ash went on to tell her that, unlike the Midwest operations, Wyoming ranches like West Ranch had livestock spread out over thousands of acres. A routine check could take hours, or even days. But Ash assured Sassy they'd be back by the end of the afternoon.

"I asked the cook to box up a few lunches for us, and some bottled sodas and waters," Ash said, dangling the keys.

"Will you let me drive the ATV?" Sassy asked, looking up at him.

"Sure, just as soon as I want to end up on a rock, like the last car you drove," Ash said, putting the keys in the pocket of his jeans.

Sassy laughed.

"That incident says more about Wyoming than my driving," she said.

"I'll tell you what," Ash said, "there's a stretch up by the pass with a shallow creek and low hills—you can drive all you like once we get up there."

"Well," Sassy said, considering the offer, "I prefer to drive in boulder fields where the sheep dart in front of me, but okay. Deal."

An hour later, after yelling a back-and-forth conversation to each other, Sassy shouted the word *stop* to Ash, and he pulled the ATV over under the shade of a large aspen. She slowly swung her legs over the open doorway and stepped onto the sagebrush covered ground.

Stretching, and enjoying the quiet of the air with the motor shut off, she smiled at Ash.

"You know, they have this thing back home in vehicles, called *shocks*. They help absorb the bumps and the ruts much better than my backside."

"It's a little bumpy, I'll give you that," Ash said, trying not to stare at the way Sassy's hands massaged the beautiful aching curves hugged by thin and faded jeans.

"You've been giving me *that* since we left the office, and I just need a little break. I can't believe we're still on West land, way out here."

Ash got out and together they looked at the full expansive view.

"Amazing here, isn't it?" Ash asked, and Sassy nodded. "We're not far from the heifer. This is as good a place as any for our picnic."

Sassy got the blanket from the back and spread it under a tree while Ash fetched the boxed lunches and drinks. They sat down, choosing to face the mountains and the gorge in the far distance.

"Great idea," Sassy said with a smile, eating her sandwich.

Ash smiled.

"It's not a fancy second date, but..."

"Whoa there, cowboy," Sassy cut him off. "You think that tour of the town was a date? That was you, being a good neighbor. And this here is a working lunch."

"Good neighbor, huh?" Ash challenged back, nudging her with his shoulder. "I nearly kissed you in the art gallery."

"I know," Sassy said quietly, and smiled.

"Would you have minded?"

"Who's to say?"

"You," Ash said with a smile—it was the same one he gave her when he kissed her boo boo, and just about made Sassy faint backwards onto the blanket.

She leaned back on her elbow and took him in. He seemed to be waiting for something from her—permission maybe to kiss her now, or validation of the near kiss in the gallery. It would change everything for her, she knew. As the breeze moved her hair around her shoulders, she looked over at Ash's piercing eyes.

The contours of his face were new to him, she guessed. Just as the river chiseled features into the gorge over the centuries, Ash's face was being carved by life and by time, and he was breathtaking. The seriousness of his gaze made her feel very small, yet being the object of his attention caused her heart to race and constrict.

She saw his forearms, and the muscles that ran from the bone on his wrist to his elbows were capable of both catching her, and removing the smallest of splinters with ease. As Sassy admired the ropey contours, and wondered how it would feel to have his arms wrapped around her, Ash leaned back on the blanket next to her.

A breeze blew a few ringlets from the top of her head onto her cheek, and Ash reached over and gently brushed them from her face. She closed her eyes with a flutter, focusing on the sensation—his fingers were warm on her skin and his caress was gentle. She could hear him exhale as he traced the edge of her jaw, and Sassy blushed at the unbidden thoughts.

"Why did you come all the way to Wyoming?" Ash asked in a rumbly whisper.

If only you knew, Sassy thought.

CHAPTER 28

"I'll ask you again. Who are you, Sassy?"

"What do you mean, Ash?"

The two were reclining on the blanket, staring up at the sky beyond the mountain range. Neither one anxious to get back in the ATV, or, it seemed, anxious to move away from each other.

"I mean, I've called you Bo Peep, and Scarlett O'Hara. We've joked around and had a few meals, but I don't know much about you, or why you're here. Rowdy and Gunnar said you were persistent about working at West Ranch this summer."

Sassy just shrugged.

"There's no mystery. West Ranch is the biggest and best, and you have to be persistent to get the job you want in life. Especially if you don't get one handed to you on a silver platter after graduation."

Ash frowned at her comment, but chose his response carefully.

"I've been handed a few silver platters in recent years, it's true. There've been a few hard knocks along the way, too. But you're making this about me, and it's not."

"There's nothing to solve. I'm an accounting grad with an interest in managing a ranch—the experience here is priceless. I'll be able to go anywhere and work after this summer."

Rolling towards Ash, Sassy propped her head up with a bent arm. Ash did the same. They were just inches away as they lay on their sides, facing each other.

"So you plan on leaving." He stated this, more than asked.

"I'm not planning anything just yet," Sassy said with an unmistakable edge in her voice. "I'll have to leave if I'm not offered a job, but I'm not sure I'd stay, anyway. There's a lot of unknowns, Ash."

Ash clenched his jaw as he looked over her shoulder at the mountain peaks, then back to Sassy and her golden hair. Her eyes were dark with mystery and a little unease.

She couldn't meet his stare. Distractedly, she looked down and began picking small leaves off the blanket and tossing them behind her. She was so beautiful, Ash thought, and he'd made her angry with his questions. As if reading his mind, she met his gaze again.

"And by the way, Ash West," she said quietly, "what makes you think a person—a girl—ought to share her whole life story the first time she meets a guy? There's a lot I don't know about you, and yet I'm willing to let it all unfold."

"Fair enough…" Ash attempted to appease Sassy. "I guess because I rescued you…"

"Rescued?"

"Well, yes…" He sounded unsure of himself now.

"What's so *noble* about stopping on a deserted road, simply because you can't go any further with a flock of sheep in your way? What's noble about being able to get cell phone reception? You're going to have to work a little harder to be my hero, Ash West."

She was right, he knew. If he wanted her to open up more, he would have to be patient and tread carefully. Sassy was an employee of the ranch, and he had to protect their reputation, and hers. But the closer he was to her, the harder it was to be cautious.

"I'm sorry, Sassy," Ash whispered. "I'm being selfish, wanting to know where you're going to be when the summer's over. I have a thing, I guess, about people in my life leaving."

Her face softened.

The two were so close. Ash reached his hand up and one by one, moved thick strands of curls from her neck to the back of her shoulder. She could feel every nerve ending as his fingers tenderly brushed her skin.

They were close enough to feel the warm breath as each other spoke.

"I don't know where I'll be, Ash," Sassy whispered, helplessly frozen in place by his hypnotic touch. "I wish I could tell you."

"Then tell me," Ash whispered back.

"I can't," she managed.

Not yet, she thought.

"Even this morning," she said, "I didn't know I'd be spending the day up on this hill, with you by my side."

Her eyes reluctantly pulled away from his own—*she was getting hopelessly caught up in him*—only to rest on the pearl snaps of his shirt. Her eyes traveled slowly down each one to where the hem hung open, revealing a few inches of his tanned torso. Her hand was so close, and when she reached over and lightly touched his warm skin with the tiny tip of her finger, Ash gasped.

"Sassy," he choked out.

"Shh," she managed, "no more questions."

Watching her eyes for permission, Ash found it instead upon her lips. As she tilted her head towards him, they parted in a sweet smile.

He closed the gap between their lips until his rested upon hers. Moving his free hand to her waist, Ash gently kissed Sassy, lingering until they were breathing in sync, and until she inched closer towards him on the warm blanket. Ash should have pulled away, but he didn't. He could feel her long eyelashes flutter against his face like butterflies, and practically hear her heartbeat getting louder—or maybe that was his own.

After a few minutes, Sassy moved the arm that held her head up, lowering herself slowly to the quilt where she lay on her back. Ash's mouth stayed with hers, and he tucked his free arm under her shoulder, where he could feel the softness of her hair as they kissed.

Her lips tasted warm and sweet. Like ripe berries dipped in sweet honey, then dipped in an electric current that ran from her mouth and through his entire body—down to the boots on his toes.

CHAPTER 29

"*S*hoot!"

Gunnar was sorting through ranch mail a few days later, next to Sassy's desk. It was mid-morning and most everyone else had left the building.

At his tone, Sassy glanced up from her spreadsheets, wondering what was wrong. She'd been working on numbers since sunup, and needed to pull her eyes away. That was the thing about numbers—they had to go somewhere to mean something, and it could be tedious work.

"What's up?" She asked, standing to stretch, then walking over to fill her coffee cup.

"Kat's been waiting for this piece of West Foundation mail, but it came here by mistake. I was just heading out to the east pens though," Gunnar said. "Sassy, would you mind driving this over to the big house for me?"

Adrenaline shot through Sassy's body at the opportunity, dropped right in her lap.

At last.

"Sure... sure I can do that, Gunnar," she said, fumbling the words in her eagerness.

"I imagine you wouldn't mind a break from the computer," he said agreeably. "No one person should spend such a beautiful summer day in Wyoming in front of a screen, and that's not our intention. So if you wouldn't mind the distraction, I'd be obliged."

Sassy took the mail from Gunnar and smiled. He was consistently one of the nicest men she'd ever met. All the West men were easy-going and polite; tall and handsome too.

"I don't mind at all," she said. "I'll go right now."

"Take one of the Jeeps, why don't you," he said, tipping his hat before leaving.

Breathe, Sassy told herself as she walked outside. She didn't want to be anxious or winded as she drove a ranch vehicle, or when meeting Kat West again.

SHE'D MET HER ONCE, WEEKS BEFORE, WHEN THE ENTIRE FAMILY CAME to an event designed to kick off summer activities. Sassy shook hands with Liu and Colton, a striking young couple. Unlike the cowboys, he wore a polo shirt with West Development embroidered on the chest, and mirrored sunglasses atop his spiked hair. Liu was very hip with her maternity sundress and sleek black hair. Sassy noticed how Colton kept his hand lightly on Liu's back as they moved around the room, and was touched by his caring and protective gestures.

Pike and Paislee were also very nice. Paislee wore a short bohemian linen dress with perfect makeup and silver jewelry, and a diamond-studded watch. Their two children seemed very close in age. At first glance, the little girl looked as though she belonged with Liu. But Paislee's attentiveness left no doubt as to who her mama was.

The little boy, Ford West, was a blonde mini-me of his daddy, Pike —the famed artist. There were a few of his paintings in the Arts and Culture Center that Ash took her to, and while Sassy was no expert, even she could see that Pike was gifted. Different from his stockier brothers, Pike was long and lean with more of a Nordic look than the others. Freda had said that Ridge's first wife was Scandinavian, so that made sense.

Ridge was there with Casey, his bride of only a few years. The two were all smiles as they went around the room. Sassy saw Ridge fill his small plate with tacos and other goodies from the commissary table, while Casey "edited," exchanging a few cheesy treats with carrot sticks and an apple.

And then there was Kat.

From a distance, Sassy watched her enter the room with an expectant grin like a *grande dame*—the hostess and matriarch of the ranch. Even though Casey was married to Ridge, Freda told her that Kat was large and in charge.

Standing at the back of the room, Sassy could see Kat was beautiful. From the twinkle in her eyes to her confidence level (which seemed off the charts) Kat West kept one manicured hand on her husband Gunnar, and extended another to each and every ranch hand and cowboy as if being introduced to royalty. She had grace and style, but worked hard to make everyone feel welcome.

"Sassy, why you hiding over there? Come on over and say hi," Gunnar called out to her, leaving her no choice but to come forward and face her at last.

"Hello," Sassy said quietly, "it's so nice to meet you." She worked hard to keep her hand from trembling with moderate success.

"Sassy," Kat said, almost fumbling over the name. She stopped mid-shake, and held the girl's hand as she searched her eyes for recognition. "Have I met you before? You seem so familiar to me."

And then, to Sassy's horror, Kat's eyes grew big and her smile faltered slightly.

"Nope."

Sassy pulled her hand away and forced her smile to widen, to compensate for Kat's own.

"She's never been anywhere near Wyoming before," Gunnar told his wife with a small laugh. "But she's doing a fine job getting our records in order, and clearing muddy creek beds with Ash in her spare time."

Gunnar tried to move Kat on.

"Darlin', you remember Red's nephew, Wayne, don't you?"

Kat's eyes remained fixed. Sassy was used to stares, and took Kat's in stride. It was a good first encounter, she thought, and had been trying to engineer a second. So far, Ash wasn't as much help as she'd hoped.

Gunnar, however, made it easy with one simple request.

CHAPTER 30

"*Oh* Lordy, what have I gone and done, what am I doing here?"
Sassy eyed the ranch house from the open-top Jeep as she
slowly approached.

Kat was waiting on this mail, but she couldn't seem to make the
car go any faster than five miles per hour. Any slower and she'd be
going backwards—part of her wanted to do just that. Turn the other
way and drive through the night back to her home, and her mother.

Hearing her heart pound, Sassy took a few cleansing breaths, then
guided the Jeep to the circular driveway near the covered front door.

The front of the ranch house made it appear almost normal in size,
though still quite elegant with its iron and wood beams. But Ash had
pointed out the back of the house that day they went to the creek, and
it was like an iceberg. Most of the house was built into the bluff and
hidden from view.

From the back, it looked more like a conference center with wings,
decks, and massive picture windows. Sassy thought she could slip in
one of the lower doors and never be noticed for weeks in such a place.

Surely Kat must have a mighty league of support staff to keep such
a place so pristine. The landscaping alone looked like it was ready for
a magazine photo shoot.

As she parked, Sassy thought about her own family home in south Illinois. It was almost ridiculous that her mother had a housekeeper and gardener, but then again, she couldn't picture her mother doing much except flipping through magazines. And they had the money.

"Whatever makes your mama happy," her daddy would say, indulgently. He was that way with Sassy, too, though seemed to have higher expectations of his daughter than his wife.

"Whatever makes you stronger, smarter, and more prepared," he would say as a barometer for her interests.

"Prepared for what?" Sassy would ask when she was young, only to receive a sad smile in return by way of an answer.

For this, she knew now, walking towards the massive double door. For a time when she was a fatherless child; practically alone in the world and tasked with carrying out her daddy's final wish.

CHAPTER 31

*K*at didn't bother to hide her surprise at seeing Sassy standing in the doorway.

"Oh, hello Sassy," she said, coolly.

"Gunnar asked me to come by," Sassy hurriedly explained, "to bring your mail."

Still knitting her brow, Kat opened the door a little wider.

"Come on in."

Stepping into the impressive foyer, Sassy exclaimed at the antler chandelier overhead, and *oohed* a little at the inlaid marble flooring. Her eyes caught the family portraits on the wall and the stone fireplace in the background, at the far end of the connecting great room.

As Sassy took in the visual treats, Kat seemed to be watching her closely.

"Let's go in the kitchen," Kat said, "you look thirsty, and a little pale."

"It must be the altitude still," Sassy said to a skeptical Kat. "I've been dizzy at times."

Kat nodded and turned so Sassy would follow. "There's other things that cause dizziness, you know," said the doctor. "If it doesn't go away soon, you might want to have a physical exam and some bloodwork."

"I'll keep that in mind," Sassy said, wondering what Kat was implying. People tended to make assumptions about pretty girls—*if she's dizzy, she must be preggers, right?* She was guilty until proven innocent, apparently. Sassy expected more from Kat, and if this is what she had been thinking, was more than a little disappointed.

Little did anyone know, and it was nobody's business, that Sassy kept men at arm's length as a rule. A rule she had broken for Ash, whose kiss she did not regret and could still taste. Being on West Ranch was intoxicating for Sassy, for many reasons now. It could be that Ash was getting tangled up in her complex emotions.

But honestly, Sassy thought, before long, she'd be gone and none of it would matter.

Minutes later, the two were perched on stools against a marble kitchen island so big it could land a small airplane.

"I'm sure you hear it all the time, but this house is amazing," Sassy managed, after gratefully sipping the cold lemonade. The bracing tang of the drink revived her senses.

"Yes, it is amazing," Kat said. "I never thought I'd be living in such a place, but it's become home to me."

"Did you... grow up in Wyoming?" Sassy ventured, already knowing the answer.

"No. Northern Illinois," Kat said, watching the girl closely. "Not far from Wisconsin. You?"

"Southern Illinois," Sassy said. "Close to the Missouri border."

"Ah," Kat nodded, eyeing Sassy with interest. "You're a long way from home." And then, "Why did you come here, Sassy?"

Sassy felt her heartrate increase at the question as blood drained from her head—she thought she might faint, but forced herself to reach down and lift the glass. With a trembling hand, she focused her energy on stilling the shaking ice cubes and taking another tart sip. This was the opening she'd been looking for with Kat, and opened her mouth to answer.

"I came to tell..."

"Mommy, Mommy," a sharp little voice interrupted Sassy before she could say more. A child came running into the room, excitedly holding a book.

"Willow…" Kat started to say.

"Mommy, I can read this one all by myself!"

"That's great sweetie," Kat said, "you can read it to me in a minute, but first, do you see we have company?"

"Oh, hi," the girl said to Sassy, rallying admirably to gain her composure. Sassy was sure that the girl's parents were raising her as heir to a vast fortune and responsibility—*of whom much is given, much will be required*, or so goes the scripture.

"Willow, this is miss Sassy. She works in the ranch office, and is visiting us from the state of Illinois—the same state…" and then, Kat looked up at Sassy with a jerk before continuing, only this time, there was a dawn of recognition in her eyes, "…the same state I grew up in."

"How do you do, Willow," Sassy said with grace equal to Kat's own. "It's nice to meet you. And you're reading books already? You must be very smart."

Sassy had never been around many children in her life, but knew from her father's example never to point out a little girl's beauty.

Nobody can take credit for their God-given looks, he'd say; *encourage their accomplishments and their mind instead.* Which is how he raised Sassy.

"Would you like me to read to you?" Willow asked, about to hand her book to Sassy. Mama Kat intervened and took the book from the little hands.

"Sassy needs to get back to the office, Willow," Kat said, "and I need to open my mail. We'll see our guest out, and then read a few books together, okay?"

"Okay Mommy," Willow said, "bye Miss Sassy."

"Bye Willow," Sassy said as she stood up to go, sensing Kat's hot gaze even without looking. "Thanks for the lemonade, Mrs. West… Kat."

Kat nodded, still holding a frown on her face as she gave her head a little shake and led Sassy to the door. There was no fond farewell, or *"come back soon."* Moments later, as she walked to the Jeep, Sassy flinched as she felt as much as heard the large wood and iron door close hard behind her.

And a feeling of foreboding in the pit of her stomach.

"WHEW, I WOULD NOT WANT TO BE ON THE WRONG SIDE OF KAT WEST," Sassy said to herself as she made her way back. Kat had done all the right things, as the matriarch of one of the biggest ranches in Wyoming.

Nobody could accuse her of being inhospitable.

And yet...

There were no warm and fuzzies awaiting Sassy in the big house. Instead of feeling welcomed, Sassy felt as though Kat was biding her time and watching the clock; anxious to escort her guest out the door, and toss her back into the dry hot Wyoming sun.

Could she blame her? Kat was a busy doctor and mother, as well as wife to Gunnar West. Individually, these were all full-time jobs. Then there was the foundation. Sassy knew the West Foundation, led by Kat West, actively raised and dispersed funds to schools, shelters, and individuals in need—it was all there in the foundation's social media posts.

The look on the students' faces when they all received new laptops from the West Foundation is something I'll never forget, a teacher from the high school posted.

Kat West was a godsend, posted another local family, after their home was flooded by the West River in springtime, and they had their temporary housing paid for.

The posts impressed Sassy, and filled her with hope that Kat would warm up to her before summer's end.

"Be a godsend for me, Kat West," Sassy said out loud, as a plea and a prayer. "There's nobody else."

CHAPTER 32

"*H*e likes you."

"Stop it."

"I won't. He *likes* you, likes you."

Sassy and her roomie were fixing their supper after a long day on the ranch. Freda had been helping Ash spread feed for the herds, and was filled with observations and insight.

"Ash wouldn't stop asking me questions about you," Freda continued. *"What's it like to live with Sassy? Do you think she has a boyfriend back home?"*

"He did not ask you that!" Sassy was now fully engaged in the conversation.

"Oh, he did too," Freda told her.

"I'll kill him," Sassy said under her breath.

"What's that," Freda asked, "did you say you'll *kiss* him... again?"

Sassy turned towards Freda, who was having way too much fun at her expense, and searched her face. Did Ash kiss and tell? Sassy didn't think he would, but how else would Freda know? She hadn't said a thing.

Freda, looking like a cat that swallowed the canary, dropped her smug look and set down her plate.

"Oh come on Sassy, lighten up. I'm only teasing," Freda scolded her roommate. "Stop taking this so personally—you can dish out the *Jim Tim's* all day long, but can't take teasing when it's about Ash West. I think you like him too. Why won't you tell me?"

Sassy dropped her shoulders and set her own plate down.

"I like him a little," Sassy said at last, "and he did kiss me once. It was nice."

Technically it was once, but Sassy didn't say that it lasted a very. Long. Time.

"I thought so," Freda said, triumphantly. "You both have been going around with your head in the clouds for days, just like I did when I first fell in love."

"I'm not in love, Freda," Sassy insisted. "It's all complicated. More than you know."

"Then tell me."

"Not yet," Sassy said. "Now, let's eat your mac and cheese. It's way better hot, before it starts congealing and sticking together into gooey and disgusting... *mac balls.*"

Freda expelled a hard and surprised laugh at her friend's comment and wrinkled nose, taking all the tension in the room with it.

CHAPTER 33

"*B*ut, why?"

"No real reason, I'd just prefer it."

"You'd prefer that Sassy not come to the house again—did she steal an ashtray? Was she rude to you? Tell me why, Kat." Gunnar was pressing Kat for a more definitive answer than the one she'd given, which was a non-answer.

"If there's mail at the office that I need, I can come get it. Or you can just bring it home, okay?" Kat was trying to steer the conversation, Gunnar knew. He wasn't letting her off the hook. They both knew that at the hospital, with her Director of Infectious Diseases hat on, Kat was used to having her orders followed without question.

"When I was growing up, there were cowboys in the house all the time, coming and going," Gunnar told Kat. "Of course, my mother was more involved in the day-to-day running of the ranch, and the house was still being built and all. It was chaos, I'll admit. And I wouldn't recommend it."

Gunnar smiled over at his wife. They were sitting on the deck overlooking the gorge. The evening had gone cool, and Kat was curled up with a wool throw on her legs. They both held a cup of hot coffee in their chilled hands.

"Did she let just anybody in the house, with small children and all?" Kat wanted to know.

"Well yes, but Daddy never hired just *anybody*—same as now. There was a time when cowboys were recruited at the blacksmith in town, or at the general store. Just like when my great grandmother Addie recruited Pickford West."

"Recruited? Picked him up, you mean," Kat said with a laugh.

"Well, she did marry him pretty fast," Gunnar said, "made an honest cowboy out of him."

"Your point being?"

"My point is this—our cowboys may seem like a rag tag bunch, but each and every person working on this ranch has been screened, with a complete background check. We know everybody who comes through our gates, and you have to trust I'd never send anyone to our doors who means any harm. You and Willow are my precious jewels."

"I know," Kat said. "But Gunnar, you can't screen for ulterior motives. And my woman's intuition is screaming at me to circle the wagons and keep her outside of *us*. My over-protective radar is going off like a siren, saying Sassy what's-her-name has a motive. I just don't know yet what it is."

Gunnar nodded as he listened.

"By the way," Kat turned to her husband, "what is Sassy's last name?"

"I don't recall," Gunnar said, "nothing special; nothing that rang a bell when I heard it—if I did hear it, that is. Now you've got me questioning everything."

"Good."

"I suppose. And this is your home. I won't send her to the house if you're uncomfortable. Though my own intuition is perfectly at ease having Sassy on the ranch. She's smart and funny; nice too. And I think Ash might be smitten with her."

"I was afraid of that."

"Consider that fear founded."

Gunnar and Kat turned towards the setting sun over the gorge and took sips of their coffee. In the silence, they could hear the bugling of a bull moose, and the screeching of a hawk as it swooped over the river.

Nighttime was their favorite time together. Willow was fast asleep and the cattle were lowing softly along the wide-open range. Most nights, one of the two would eventually reach for the other in the dark, and they would wordlessly make their way to bed. There, they melted into kisses that tasted like warm moonlight and embraced each other with eager loving arms.

This might have been one of those nights, except Gunnar had to wrap up their conversation about Sassy, and he regretted what he had to say. He suspected it would set Kat in a foul mood.

"There's one more thing, darlin', that I have to come clean about."

Kat looked over, curiously. She didn't like the tone of his voice, and it put her on edge.

"There's one thing I haven't told you about Sassy," Gunnar continued.

"What's that?"

"There is something about her... that reminds me... of you."

CHAPTER 34

"Kat!"

Rowdy seemed surprised to see his cousin's wife in the ranch office. It was after lunch and the place was deserted—no end of chores today. Even Sassy left with Ash and Freda to go repair fences up by the pass. A fallen tree limb had taken some posts with it and if they didn't hurry, some of the West cattle would be making a clean getaway.

He expected everyone to be gone all afternoon, and looked forward to catching up on some ordering and other paperwork.

"Gunner's not here, Kat," Rowdy said. "He went into town with Gray to pick up engine parts."

"Hey Rowdy, I wasn't looking for Gunnar. Mind if I sit down for a minute?"

Rowdy gestured to a chair, then got up to go fill his coffee mug. He'd get some for Kat, too, without being asked. She had uncharacteristic lines on her forehead, and dark circles under her eyes. The woman had not slept well, he surmised.

"Here, Kat," he said, mug in hand. "I brought you a few cookies, too. You look like you could use them."

"That bad, huh?"

"Let's just say, I've seen you looking happier," Rowdy said.

She gave a short laugh and accepted his offerings.

"A hundred years ago, these would be shots of whiskey," she said.

"Ah, but cookies work faster for what ails you," he said, "without the hangover."

"In that case, *cheers*," Kat said, lifting a cookie as in a toast, before taking a big bite. After a few sips of the hot coffee, Kat seemed to be avoiding the reason she came.

"Rowdy, I'm hearing a rumor that you're a little sweet on a local girl."

Rowdy blushed and shrugged.

"Is Gunnar talking in his sleep again? You know you can't trust that gossip."

Kat smiled, though her efforts looked painful.

"I have more than one reliable source, Rowdy," she said. "But whatever you tell me, I'll keep to myself."

"In that case, I have been out a time or two with Daisy Shire, from the Painted Bird Gallery in town." Rowdy's grin broadened as he spoke. "She's awfully pretty, and probably too smart for the likes of this cowboy. But she seems to enjoy my company, and that makes me lucky."

Kat nodded.

"Daisy's a fine one, Rowdy. One of my first true friends when I came to town. And knowing you as I do, I'd say she's pretty lucky also."

"Well that's nice of you to say," Rowdy said quietly.

"I have to warn you though, she does have one fault, and it's a big one."

"What fault is that?" Rowdy frowned in surprise at Kat.

"Her twin sister."

Before Kat moved to town, Gunnar had a girlfriend named Darlene Shire—Daisy's twin. Thankfully, Darlene moved away to make a name for herself as a journalist, and dumped Gunnar before she left. By the time she realized her mistake and came back to town to marry Gunnar West, he'd fallen in love with Kat during a hospital quarantine.

Darlene high-tailed it out of town again, and rarely made it back home. But Kat could never shake the similarity between the two Shire sisters, even though she adored Daisy.

"But if it gets serious, Rowdy, then I'll get over it," Kat told him.

Rowdy gave her a compassionate smile.

"Get over it, Kat."

After another sip of coffee, Rowdy set his mug down.

"What brings you here?"

"Your intern, Sassy," Kat said, simply. "I need to know her last name."

Rowdy looked puzzled.

"I don't think it's a secret," he said, "I just can't remember off the top of my head. I can ask her when she returns..."

"No!" Kat said too sharply. "Don't ask. Look in her personnel file and just tell me, please."

At Kat's tone, Rowdy stood and walked to a file cabinet. After a few seconds of searching, he pulled out a manilla folder and opened it up. Then he closed it again and returned to his seat, where Kat was waiting.

"Tate," he said, "Sassy Tate."

One word—that one name—made Kat's head jerk back in shock, and the room spin.

"*Kat?* What's wrong?" Rowdy was half standing, ready to catch Kat if she fell out of the chair and onto the hard floor. "You look like you've seen a ghost."

"I... have."

CHAPTER 35

*K*at was only 14 when her father, Jack Tate, left her and her mother to fend for themselves. The image of her mother running after him as he loaded his suitcase in the car was forever burned in her memory, along with the heartbreak and sadness that lasted in their house for years.

What was worse, Kat abandoned her mother, too.

Unable to bear Trudy's grief, Kat buried herself in books, school clubs and honors classes—then medical school and a residency at the Chicago hospital. Kat rarely went home when she was an hour away by train, and never went back now that she lived in Wyoming.

Of course, her mother was always welcome to visit the ranch and came twice a year to see little Willow.

Finally, with Gunnar's help, and a good therapist in West Gorge, Kat had been able to quiet the ghosts. That is, until the legacy of Jack Tate reared its ugly head again in the form of the beautiful Sassy Tate —who must be her...

Could that be?

She knew there was something that unsettled her about the girl, and yet, something about her looked familiar. Sassy had an uncommon beauty, but also a dark and piercing confidence in her eyes that she'd seen before, in her own father.

Their father.

Her thoughts were spinning.

She had a sister; a sister who knew who she was. That meant Jack talked about her—the father that abandoned her knew who and where she was, and obviously… *what?* Sent the girl as an envoy to mend fences? Ask for forgiveness… for money?

Absurd. Audacious. Presumptuous. Impossible.

Never send a child to do a man's job, Jack.

Kat shook her head to clear her wildly swimming thoughts. She didn't want to reconcile with Jack. She didn't want to meet Sassy's mother, Sugar *Tate*—a gold digger who stole her dad and ruined her family. And Kat certainly didn't want a relationship with Sassy Tate, the spawn of such low-life people. The girl was a deceitful opportunist who wormed her way into the ranch and Kat's new *real* family under false pretenses.

Taking a deep breath, Kat stood up and pulled her slumped shoulders back into *badass* position where they belonged. She was a department head at the hospital, head of a charitable foundation, and ran a large and imposing ranch home. Her husband and daughter adored her, and she had the love and respect of a growing family. Kat wouldn't let the memories of a negligent father reduce her to a puddle of pain and emotion—those days were over.

Feeling stronger, Kat looked at Rowdy, who'd been standing close by with concern.

"Fire her," she said, walking out.

CHAPTER 36

The following Saturday, Sassy opened her front door to find a bouquet of sunflowers in a vase, a sack of still-warm bagels, and a note.

It's presumptuous to ask you on a first date today with so little notice. But if you're free, I'd love to take you to the gorge, then out for a late lunch. If you're sitting on your porch at 11 wearing sensible shoes and real clothes, then we're on. - Ash

What to do, what to do?

Sassy already accomplished her first goal, without Ash's help. That was getting into the house at West Ranch and seeing Kat West. The ice was broken. Though judging from the look on Kat's face, her icy demeanor was only growing colder—for no apparent reason.

Kat gave her the opening she was looking for to broach a terribly sensitive topic, but then little Willow interrupted them.

Willow.

Sassy hadn't thought much beyond Kat. But the child added a new dimension to her secret—the secret she carried with her this past year, and brought all the way from Illinois. Willow was smart and lovely, and Sassy felt an undeniable connection to the girl.

It was a blood connection, she realized. Something she had very little of.

Looking at the clock, Sassy could see it was past ten, so she needed to hop in the shower and get ready for Ash. Of course she would go to the gorge with him. Freda left for Lander again, and there was nobody else to hang out with. All the other ranch hands had family in the area and weekends filled with horseback riding, ATV exploring and hiking. Some were heading to Yellowstone to camp, or to Jackson Hole to whitewater raft the Snake River.

On Fridays, everyone said their goodbyes as Sassy waved.

Bye Sassy, have a fun weekend.

But nobody asked if she had anything to do, or would care to join them. Nobody, that is, except Ash West. He seemed to be the one person who understood how alone she was. Even Freda hadn't invited her to Lander again—but why should she? Who would want a third wheel on hot summer dates with Jim Tim?

Especially such a distracting third wheel, Sassy knew. She wasn't being vain, only realistic. Sassy knew how she appeared to men. They made assumptions about her, she understood. And they wouldn't believe her if she told them she'd only ever kissed a boy or two. She vowed to be even more discerning now that her father had died. Sassy always felt safe in the world knowing her father was alive and well, and looking after her. Now, all she had was her mother. And Lord knew, Sugar Tate was nobody's bodyguard. Not even her daughter's.

"Oh, quit being so stuck up and just go out with him, Sassy," Sugar would say if a man paid her any attention. "He looks like fun."

"That's the *problem*, Mother," Sassy would counter.

It was only a matter of time, Sassy knew, before Sugar would find another man to fill Jack's void. Sugar didn't need any man's money, but she did crave attention and adoration. Sassy also came to understand why her father separated his wife's finances from his daughter's, making it impossible for any future husband to have a claim on Sugar's money. Or for Sugar to have a claim on Sassy's inheritance.

Jack knew them both well.

They were all set up for life, the way he wanted them to be. Sassy couldn't help but wonder if Jack also took care of Kat, but that line of questioning would have to wait.

CHAPTER 37

Five minutes past eleven in the morning, Ash West pulled up into the driveway of his bungalow in downtown West Gorge, happy to see his next-door neighbor sitting on the porch. Like him, she was wearing board shorts, river sandals, and a tee shirt. They both had reflective sunglasses hanging from their necks, and a fleece pullover within reach.

"Ah, I see you got the dress code memo," Ash said from the open top of his Jeep.

"As did you," Sassy smiled as she stood.

"Not your usual date attire, I'm sure," he said.

"I don't have date attire," Sassy said as she walked towards Ash, "usual or otherwise."

"That can't be true." Ash got out of the Jeep, not quite knowing what to do next. Thankfully, he remembered to walk with her to the passenger door to hold it open.

"Why can't that be true, Ash? You think I get all sorts of invitations, because of the way I look?"

Ash struggled to find a response. That's exactly what he thought, but now doubted himself as he stood with his hands on the Jeep door.

"Well... *yeah*, I guess I do think that."

"And don't you think I have any say in the matter? Or must I jump at every invitation to the movies, or the theater, or out to eat? Or into a back seat or dark hallway?"

"Gee, Sassy, I'm sorry. Really. I didn't mean to offend you. I thought I was paying you a compliment, but I can see how I misstepped."

Sassy was silent as she assessed him. He really was sorry, she could tell.

"Sorry, Ash." Her voice softened. "I didn't mean to speak so harshly. Just... don't make assumptions about me, please."

Ash nodded as he got behind the wheel. He had made assumptions. And just what did he assume? He blushed at the thought, and was ashamed of himself. He would have to tread carefully going forward.

"I think," Ash said as he pulled the car out of the driveway and started heading for the gorge, "that I automatically lumped you in the same category as all the pretty girls at the university in Michigan; the beautiful and popular girls who had somewhere to go and friends to hang out with all the time. They were always laughing in that way... that carefree way I've never been able to."

"Why can't you laugh like that, Ash?"

He shrugged, but turned to smile at Sassy.

"Life is hard—people are fragile. I don't want to be frivolous... or make a mistake that will hurt somebody else. I want to build a life where I can respect what I'm doing and have a family that I'll never leave."

"You're pretty young to have such serious goals."

"Oh, I've had these goals for a long time. The thing I've had to learn is to enjoy life's journey. Instead of going after these things like my life depended on it."

"Does it?"

"Kinda."

Sassy reached over and took his free hand in her own and he gave it a squeeze.

"Let's just enjoy the journey today, together. Like two beautiful friends who have somewhere to go, and someone to hang out with."

CHAPTER 38

"*And* my backside still hurts when it rains!"

Sassy laughed at Ash's colorful tales of learning to ride a horse on the ranch. She had been walking in front of him on the hiking trail along the gorge.

"I can't believe a horse threw you when you were a kid," she said. "It's my worst fear."

"Maybe you picked the wrong guy to teach you how to be a cowgirl." Behind her, Ash wore a backpack filled with water, snacks and sunscreen. "I can ride a horse, but no one would mistake me for someone born in the saddle."

"I'm hoping to be on a horse before summer's over." Sassy kept her eyes on the trail, with one hand steady on a hiking stick. "But I confess, I'm more than a little intimidated. Horses are awfully big."

"When I first came to the ranch, I had to learn everything," Ash said. "Horse riding, fence fixing, herd feeding—everything was new to me. But my dad and brothers were patient."

"The Wests must be a special family to have taken you in as a teen."

Ash merely nodded, and pointed in the direction of the river, which was getting louder as they hiked.

"They are special; they're my family now. I shudder to think what would have become of me if I kept on my own path. I'd be a runaway, at the mercy of strangers. Or in jail."

Sassy stopped walking and turned to face Ash. As they stood still in the forest, the sound of rushing water was nearly deafening.

"Is that why you came back after college, Ash?"

"Yep," Ash nodded. "I can find a job anywhere, I reckon. But family... I won't ever take my family for granted. If they were farmers, I'd be planting corn. If they owned a grocery store, I'd be stocking cans. But as it is, I'm a rancher. Just like Gunnar."

Sassy searched his eyes.

"Where do I fit into your perfect ranching future, if I head home, that is?"

Ash looked puzzled. "Well, you tell me. You're the one who pursued West Ranch; you came after it like raindrops divebombing a puddle, so I hear."

Sassy looked miffed.

"Well that may be, but I came after a job, not after *you*, Ash West. This," Sassy gestured with her arms at the trail around them, "is all your doing."

"Okay, I don't know where you fit it with me. Or how I fit in with you—you're a mystery to me, Sassy. All I know is that you're the best of both worlds. You are everything I love about the Midwest, right here in Wyoming. You're smart and kind, and full of life. And I can't stop thinking about your kiss."

Sassy smiled.

"Oh, did we kiss? I don't seem to recall that." Her tone and body language said otherwise as she stepped a little closer to Ash and tilted her head up towards him.

Ash grinned at her obvious flirtation. He tilted his own head so that he was facing her, and brought his lips close before whispering.

"Then let me remind you, pretty cowgirl."

"THIS IS PERFECT."

Sassy took in the scene around them with satisfaction. Ash had led them to a large rock that acted as a flat-topped ledge overlooking the gorge. Water rushed down the West River, winding between and over rocks. The land where the water flowed cut deep into the features, forming a gorge that separated the prairie and the mountains.

Ash could barely hear her, except for the fact that they sat side by side with their backs against the side of the hill, legs stretched in front of them. Ash had one arm around Sassy's waist, and pulled her as close as possible. With the other hand, he held a cracker with a slice of pepper jack cheese Sassy had handed him.

"It's a great place to picnic," he said, gesturing to the jagged rocks below, "but you wouldn't want to fall asleep here. If you rolled over, it could be your last nap."

"Then I'll stick close to you."

CHAPTER 39

"We need to talk, Kat."

Gunnar's tone was gruffer than he'd intended walking into his wife's home office unannounced. After taking off his hat, he sat down across from her in one of the brocade upholstered wing chairs and looked around the room. This had been his mother's home office years before, and her pride and joy.

Randi Lynn West made this a retreat from the dusty and rustic ranch, complete with plush white carpet and fancy chairs. It was his mother's inner sanctum, and now it was Kat's. Ridge had gifted this space to her shortly after their marriage as the most precious thing he could offer his new daughter-in-law.

Now, years later, it retained the same look; the same light and feminine fragrance.

And the same rules still applied—*enter at your own risk.*

Looking around and seeing his mother's law books on the shelves along with Kat's medical journals, Gunnar was grateful that his wife left the room as it always was, amidst the fervor of her redecorating over the past few years. He knew it was a sacrifice on Kat's part; this wasn't her style. The realization made him swallow hard and soften his tone.

He couldn't read Kat's face. She set her pencil down and folded her hands on the desk. Her eyes were guarded and her mouth set—but she was so damned beautiful that he almost lost his nerve. They had been at odd ends in the past few weeks, and this conversation wasn't going to make anything better between them. Just the opposite.

"Sweetheart..." he started again.

"Oh, it's *sweetheart* now, is it?" Kat's voice held a touch of amusement in the steel.

"It seems," Gunnar said cautiously, "that something very big is happening in your life this summer; in our lives. Looks like we got more than we bargained for when Sassy came to work at the ranch."

Kat was silent as she watched him talk.

"That's an understatement," Kat said at last.

Gunnar was treading carefully.

"I hear you paid a visit to Rowdy up at the office, and I think you put him—put us *all*—in a sticky situation, between a rock and a hard place."

"I disagree, Gunnar. *Sweetheart.*" As she spoke, Gunnar cringed. "The answer is very clear. I want Sassy Tate gone. Today. She's not good for Ash. She's not good for me. And I think we can agree that her presence hasn't done much for our marriage."

Gunnar regarded her words, and the way she spit out the word *Tate*, like venom from a snake bite. She sounded more like a prosecuting attorney than a medical doctor just now, and he wondered if she'd been reading his mother's books.

He hadn't seen his wife's hard side since their ill-fated blind date, several years earlier. It was off-putting then, but he had the choice to walk away. Which he did. If they hadn't been locked up together in a hospital quarantine for a week, he would never have seen her more vulnerable side and fallen in love.

But she had ghosts, Kat did.

She pushed them down, but they re-surfaced in ways Gunnar could see every now and then. In bad dreams and free-floating insecurities. It would be good to have them gone forever, and there was only one way that would happen. Kat needed to face Sassy and deal with the realities.

For that to happen, he would need to stand firm against his wife.

"Sorry, Kat," Gunnar said, getting up to leave. "I don't negotiate with bullies. Sassy stays.

Kat shot up from her chair in anger and surprise, but Gunnar stood his ground.

"She's not leaving the ranch on my watch, Kat," he said. "I can't fire her just because she's your long-lost sister."

"There's nothing lost about her… I was never looking for her. I didn't know she existed."

"But here she is. And she… this… isn't going away, sweetheart, so I want… I *need* you to try and figure it out."

"I'll figure it out on my own terms."

"Sometimes we don't have that luxury," he said. "If you recall, I was fighting mad when I got locked in the hospital with you during the quarantine."

Kat looked up in surprise at his words.

"But it made me face some things I'd been running from," he went on, "like how angry I was about my mother's death."

Kat was silent.

"That quarantine was a shortcut for me, painful though it was. It helped me move on. Sassy leaving now won't help you move on, Kat. I didn't engineer it, but here it is—here she is. I feel we ought to deal with what's in front of us."

"So that's it then? You're forcing me to face my past because *you* feel it's time?"

Gunnar could see that his wife was angry with him.

"I'm your husband, Kat, not your enemy, and I love you. I'm the one who holds you at night when you have nightmares. I'm the one who reassures you when you have fears and doubts. And yes, I do feel it's time," he spoke steadily. "What you do is up to you. But Rowdy and I are not going to fire Sassy before her internship ends. She's qualified to do her job, and it's not a crime to be your sister. In fact, I like her all the more for it."

"She deceived you, Gunnar—deceived us all."

"Well true, she didn't come to the ranch with guns blazing, declaring who she was. But can you blame her? Look at how you're reacting?"

"What's a normal reaction in this situation?" Kat spat at him. "I'd really like to know."

"I guess I feel sorry for her. You're practically the only family she has, since her... your... father died last year."

At that, Kat's head spun towards Gunnar and locked on his eyes.

"He *what?*"

"Wait..." he said carefully, "Sassy didn't tell you?"

"She tried to, I think."

"Your mama didn't tell you? Surely word made its way..."

"I haven't been... returning her calls." Kat's words came out in a hoarse whisper.

Gunnar nodded in stunned silence.

Good Lord.

CHAPTER 40

"Shhh, we don't want to wake anybody," Ash tugged on Sassy's hand while holding a finger to his lips. They spent the full day at the river, followed by dinner at a popular restaurant located by the trail head. The two had to wait a long time for their table, since a large wedding party occupied half the dining room.

No matter, Ash and Sassy lost track of time as they talked about all manner of subjects, such as school and work. Both avoided talk of family, for their own reasons. And food was always a safe topic—which is how they ended up in the ranch kitchen. Ash insisted Sassy try Liu's spring rolls before she let another day pass her by.

The two, who had been laughing loudly just moments ago while driving down the dark ranch road, now tried to contain their volume as they walked into the kitchen.

The only light was a soft glow illuminating the counter tops.

"Why are we here again?" Sassy giggled into Ash's shoulder.

"Spring rolls, remember? You said you were starving, and couldn't wait 'til we got back to town."

"Oh yeah," she said, in a close to normal voice.

"Shhh, you've got to keep your voice down, Sassy."

"But don't you live here?"

"Yes, I do."

Ash thought about that. He'd always have a home at the ranch, the family made that clear. But he'd been living at the bungalow in town this summer. And just like Colton, Pike, and even Ridge, it was only a matter of time before he'd find his own place.

The home on the ranch, the Big House, as the Wests called it, was becoming his home away from home, and part of him felt he was trespassing on Kat and Gunnar—especially, though he didn't know why, with Sassy in his arms.

Ash could never remember a time when his older brothers brought girls to the ranch, until they were practically wives, that is. It made him feel guilty, and he wanted to get out of there. He only hoped Sassy wouldn't ask to see his rooms, or get a grand tour in the dark. But it was exciting having her with him. It made him feel very grown up, as if he too was bringing the woman he might marry.

"I found the fridge," Sassy whispered, and tugged his hand.

Silently, the door on the sub-zero opened to reveal a platter of Liu's famous delicacies. Ash put four in his hand and turned to smile at Sassy in the dark. Her lovely features were lit by the refrigerator, and he was drawn to her smile.

"Kiss me," he whispered.

"But I'm starving," she whispered back.

"Me too," he said, quietly closing the door of the appliance.

In the dark, they drew close until her body was pressed against his own, and they held each other tight. Ash's arms wrapped around Sassy's small waist as he caressed her back.

"One spring roll for every kiss," he said, nuzzling her warm neck.

"That's bribery, but okay," she said with a gasp, as he brought his lips to her jawline and worked his way along her cheek.

Sassy inhaled sharply as she pulled him closer, hungrily searching for his mouth in the dark. When they met, Ash and Sassy were barely breathing as the sensation overtook them both. In the dark, everything around them melted away. They could only sense the warmth and taste of each other in a new and deeper way than before.

Without thought, both held each other tighter, their bodies swaying almost imperceptibly.

Nighttime kisses, they were learning, had more meaning. More power. More depth than sunlight kisses. It both intrigued and frightened them as they began to understand where kisses in the dark could lead. The tighter she gripped his shoulders, the harder Ash held onto her. His hands kneaded the muscles on Sassy's back and worked their way downward. He fairly gasped as he felt just a hint of the curves that waited below—a place his hands had no right to be, he knew.

Flashes of his room began playing in his mind, as he wondered if Sassy would go there with him. But he shook his thoughts clear, knowing what a betrayal the mere suggestion would be to Sassy. She'd told him not to make assumptions.

"We'd... better get out of here," Ash said, catching his breath, though it was hard to pull back from their embrace.

Nodding and loosening her grip, she exhaled a trembling breath, making Ash want to start all over again. He willed himself to move away.

"Let's go," Sassy whispered in his neck as she slipped her hand in his.

Quietly, they moved as one to the door to slide back under the Wyoming stars then towards their homes. Neither saw the third person in their presence; someone watching with great interest from a darkened corner of the adjacent great room.

After she was certain the pair had left, Kat exhaled raggedly, boiling with anger.

CHAPTER 41

If she's not leaving then I'm going.

Kat tried to go about her business as usual the next day, but remained red hot with rage over the continued presence of Sassy. That Gunnar and Rowdy wouldn't cut her loose from the ranch was a slap in the face, and it burned. And hurt. The ranch had become her sanctuary—her home. A place where she could put the past behind her at last and focus on what she could control, and that was her little family.

But even that didn't feel safe any longer, in light of...

The presence of Sassy on the ranch made it feel like four walls were closing in on her, even though there were thousands of acres and miles of wide-open spaces.

In blind anger, Kat stomped into her suite and threw a suitcase on the bed.

"I've got to get out of here," she said as she threw odd bits of clothing into the open bag without stopping to fold or organize anything. It didn't matter—she'd buy what she needed when she got to... *where? Where was she going?*

That didn't matter either.

Kat was distraught and didn't see or hear Willow enter the room.

The child was half cowering by the wall, looking at her mother with what could only be fear in her eyes.

"Mommy?" The small girl spoke tentatively, but it cut through the tension like a sharp knife. Kat looked over, wild eyed, which only frightened the girl. In her six years, Willow had never seen her mother as anything but calm and in control.

"Are we going somewhere Mommy?" Willow spoke again with an unmistakable tremble in her voice. "Should I get my suitcase, too?"

Kat took a sharp intake of breath at the question, blinking hard as she struggled to focus on her daughter, and her next words. Her eyes stung as she blinked away hot tears that felt salty and sharp. For a minute, she was a young girl again, watching her father pack his bags —wondering if she and her mom and dad were finally taking a family vacation, the one that had been promised for years.

Are we going somewhere, Daddy? Should I pack?

"Yes, sweetie, we're all going up to Yellowstone for a few days."

It was a deep voice. Gunnar was in the room, assessing Kat and Willow and answering.

"Willow, why don't you go pack a few toys and books, and your favorite PJs. I'll come help with the rest in a little while, after I help mommy pack."

He kissed the girl on the top of her head, and hugged her until she exhaled her fears and rewarded him with a smile and laugh. When she left, Gunnar softly closed the door.

"Where are you going, Kat?"

Gunnar was standing next to her, with concern in his eyes. He reached his hands up to her, but then dropped them again.

As in a dream, Kat shook her head. "I just have to get away. Go somewhere else."

"Do you?"

Do I?

Looking up at her husband and suddenly feeling uncertain, her anger melted and her legs gave way as she crumpled onto the edge of the bed. Gunnar fell to the carpet, kneeling next to her. He reached up again but this time he pulled her to him in a hard embrace.

Kat resisted at first, but then dropped her head onto his shoulders and cried like she hadn't in many years. Waves of pain poured from her as Gunnar simply held on, stroking her hair and holding his wife in his arms. They sat like this for a long time, Gunnar eventually reaching into his pocket to hand Kat a clean handkerchief.

At last, he pulled away to gaze into her face—red and swollen from the tears. But more appealing and beautiful than ever to him in her vulnerability.

"I promised on our wedding day that I would never leave you, nor forsake you. And I'm keeping that promise, Kat, and asking the same in return."

She regarded him thoughtfully.

Before she could speak, he went on.

"If you need to get away, then let's all go. We'll take Willow right now and leave everything for a few days—the ranch, the hospital and Sassy. But we won't leave each other. Okay? That's not who we are."

It would have been easy to say *no*; that it wasn't necessary to leave.

Only, *it so was.*

As she was debating their little trip, the rational and irrational warring inside her head, the door opened and Willow ran into the room, holding her small pink duffel bag.

"I'm ready for Yellowstone, Mommy," she said with a laugh. "I've got my bathing suit and five books, two stuffed bears and sunglasses. Oh, and a nightlight. And some candy I found from Christmas. Let's go."

Gunnar smiled and laughed, and so did Kat, he was glad to see.

"Let's go," Kat smiled as she pulled Willow into a hug. "Give me ten minutes to finish my packing and I'll be ready."

The three looked over at Kat's open suitcase, spilling over with an angry hodgepodge of wool slacks, still on the hanger, tee shirts, a pearl-buttoned riding shirt, and running shorts.

"I'll give you twenty," Gunnar said.

CHAPTER 42

"*H*mm, somehow I pictured the ranch being much bigger than this."

Erik Olsen got out of Ash's Jeep and looked at the little bungalow in town. Ash tossed Erik his duffel bag and smiled. "After we drop off your things, I'll take you out to the ranch and the gorge. But you and I will bunk here," he said. "I guarantee, the view is prettier."

Just then, Sassy and Freda pulled into the driveway next door and got out to carry in the bags from their Saturday morning grocery run.

"I see what you mean," Erik said with a smile to Ash.

"Ladies," Ash called over, "need a hand?"

"Oh, if we can clear trees from the creek and help the heifers birth their calves, I think we can manage a bag or two of noodles and bananas," Freda said with a smile in Erik's direction. She was wearing one of her roommate's sundresses with her river sandals, and a single silver bangle gleamed against the tan of her skin.

Sassy thought her roomie was looking at Ash's friend a little too long, and gave her a slight nudge with the gallon of milk in her hand.

"Move along, Freda," she said under her breath.

Ignoring her, Freda smiled even bigger, which was returned by the young man neither had met. He was as tall as Ash, with blonde wavy hair and bright blue eyes, and a deep tan of his own.

"Where are your manners, Ash?" Freda spoke.

Dropping his shoulders in resignation, Ash walked around to where Freda and Erik were standing.

"Sassy and Freda," he said, "this is Erik—my friend from Michigan. I invited him to come to the big West Ranch cookout tomorrow night, and get a taste of ranch life."

"And barbecue," Erik said. "Ash promised me dinner at a place called Red's tonight. Which sounds a whole lot better than noodles and bananas, if you two would join us."

"We'd love to," Freda spoke up. "We have no previous engagements, do we Sassy?"

Sassy looked over at Ash, who had his mouth hanging open in surprise, but not disappointment. He and Sassy shrugged and smiled at each other. They both knew his friend was expected, and figured they wouldn't see each other very much. But Erik and Freda changed all that. Their attraction to each other was immediate, and concerning, Sassy thought. Even though she'd never met the elusive Jim Tim, she thought he and Freda were a serious item. In fact, every Sunday, when Freda returned from Lander, Sassy surveyed her friend's hand for a sparkling diamond.

"Well that's settled," Ash said. "We will pick you up at six, so be hungry."

"Starving," Freda and Erik said in unison, and then laughed.

"Well, look at you, all flushed from flirting and gawking at Ash's friend," Sassy said to Freda as they walked into the house. "Truth be told, I've never seen you look more radiant."

Sassy began putting groceries away while grilling her friend.

Freda merely shrugged, but retained a private smile.

"Come on, Sassy, he's gorgeous," Freda said at last.

"So are you, Freda," Sassy countered, "but I was under the impression that you were spoken for. You weren't acting like a future missus lawyer just now."

That did it—Freda's face turned into a frown as she tossed the milk in the fridge with all the delicacy of a baseball pitch.

"James Timothy Freemont has allowed me to shlepp my sore, aching body all the way to Lander every weekend this summer," Freda said, "without making special plans for us, or welcoming me with open arms."

Sassy poured two iced lemonades and sat down at the table to listen to this new information. Freda followed suit.

"Sometimes he seems outright surprised to see me, as if he hadn't given me much thought, and it hurts my feelings. Lately I feel as if I'm throwing myself at him, which isn't at all how it was before this summer. For two years we've been scheming, and talking about how it will be after law school. Well, here it is—and *nothing*."

Freda stopped and took a sip, then set her glass down and looked at Sassy.

"My gut tells me he's a coward. Too scared to propose, and too scared to break up."

Freda's lip quivered, but then she sat up straight and looked her friend in the eye. "On the flipside, that tall beautiful Norse god who got out of Ash's Jeep made me feel pretty... and *seen*. And—don't take this the wrong way—but he was looking at me and barely noticed you, Sassy. So I'm going to enjoy tonight's date at Red's BBQ. And if he has a little sauce on those beautiful full lips of his, I may offer to kiss it off."

Smiling at her friend, Sassy nodded.

"Okay, little firecracker, let's get you all *purtee,* and go have some fun."

CHAPTER 43

*A*sh gave Erik the one-minute tour of the bungalow, and pointed him to the spare room.

"Now," Ash said with a happy grin, "let's go see the good stuff."

"The scenery can't possibly get any better than your neighbors," Erik said with a grin of his own, "but let's go."

The two filled their water bottles with ice and grabbed sunscreen and their mirrored shades for riding in the open-top Jeep. The day was sunny and warm, and Erik was glad to see Wyoming for the first time. He'd flown to Salt Lake City from Detroit the day before, then took a puddle jumper early that morning to the outskirts of West Gorge.

"Man oh man, look at those mountains. I've been stuck in Michigan way too long," Erik gushed as the two drove. Ash felt a swell of pride at his friend's words.

"Michigan is amazing—*Lake* Michigan is amazing," Ash said. "The two states are just... very different."

They took a quick detour through town to grab a sack of burgers and passed the main street, where Amber was setting a SALE sign in front of her Amber Waves storefront. Ash gave a small beep of his horn, and she smiled and waved to the boys, revealing the deep dimples on her face.

Erik whistled under his breath.

"You didn't mention how pretty the girls are in Wyoming, man," he said, giving Ash a good-natured slug to his arm. "No wonder you wanted to come back home."

Ash smiled as he drove with a burger in his hand, and gestured to the massive log and iron arches they were about to pass under, with the West Ranch insignia overhead.

"This is why I came home," he said through his mouthful of lunch.

Erik whistled again.

Minutes later, the two pulled up in front of Colton's log and stone house, where a very pregnant Liu was outside in her kitchen garden, near the tea house.

"You two look hungry," she said as they got out.

"Thanks, Liu," Ash said, "but I just came to introduce my friend from Michigan."

"Colton is at the big house, overseeing the tents for the big cookout tomorrow," Liu said. And then to Erik, "you came on a good weekend. The West Ranch cookout is the hottest ticket in town."

"I can't wait," Erik said. "But... you mean this isn't the *big house*?" He was gazing in awe at the large log structure, with several decks, levels, and outbuildings—including a full guest house the size of the Olsen family home.

Liu and Ash laughed at that.

"Oh no," Liu said, "you'll know the big house when you see it. Nice to meet you, Erik."

Continuing on the ranch road, Ash pointed out the cook house, the guest house, and some of the barns and ranch offices. They passed the family cemetery, and the pavilion where the Wests held their outdoor gatherings. There, a fleet of catering trucks were unloading and assembling tents and setting up portable structures for the party.

Ash pulled up alongside Colton, Gray and Rowdy, and introduced them to Erik.

"Gunner got off easy this year," Colton said with a laugh. "Wish I'd thought of taking an impromptu trip to Yellowstone. Didn't know we could do that during the cookout weekend."

Ash thought it was odd too, but they all knew the trip must have been important to Gunnar and Kat, or else they wouldn't have left town. Everyone in the family looked forward to the yearly event.

As the boys pulled into the circle drive of the ranch house, Erik looked at the impressive lodge pole pine entrance and nodded respectfully.

"I still don't think it's as big as..."

"Wait for it!" Ash said, taking his friend through the double doors and into the foyer. From there, they could see the massive kitchen, great room, and sweeping stone fireplace rising up nearly three stories high. Out the windows, the West River flowed and rushed out of the deep cut of the gorge, as if it was a protective moat in front of the mountain range.

An hour later, Erik was duly impressed with West Ranch. Standing in the kitchen, as Ash searched the refrigerator for the always present pitcher of fresh-squeezed lemonade, Ridge and Casey walked in.

"I thought I heard rustlers," Ridge said, clapping Ash on the back and shaking Erik's hand.

"Just rustling up something to drink," Ash said.

"Sir, ma'am," Erik greeted Ash's family. "Your ranch is just beautiful. And the view of those mountains and the gorge... why, I don't have the right words."

"It's great that you came for the cookout, Erik," Casey said warmly. "There'll be a lot of pretty girls to dance with."

"I can't wait," Erik said, "we're taking two pretty girls out to dinner tonight—Sassy and Freda; Ash's neighbors."

"Neighbors; yes. Also employees of the ranch," Ridge said with caution in his voice. "Mind your manners, lads."

"Always, sir," Erik replied sincerely.

"Very good. Very good. Now," Ridge said, "we spotted a newly born elk calf up in the foothills, by the north pasture, if you're looking for something to see. Mama won't let you get too close, but it's worth the trek."

"Thanks, Dad."

Ash hugged Ridge and Casey, who once again welcomed Erik to their home.

As they got back in the Jeep, Ash turned to his friend.

"So, what's it going to be? Hiking by the gorge? Fly fishing in the river? Horseback riding? We've got all afternoon."

"Everything," Erik said. "Let's do the full *Wyoming*."

CHAPTER 44

*I*t took Kat an entire day until she was finally ready to talk.

Since arriving at the park, they'd spent hours hiking along the geyser basin, to Yellowstone Falls and the mud pots.

"Pee you!" Willow held her nose against the sulphur smell.

They drove amongst the roaming buffalo, and spotted moose, deer and elk. They even saw a glimpse of a black bear way up on a hill. Kat was quiet as the threesome enjoyed the waterfalls, and swam in a natural swimming hole in Firehole Canyon. Like a zombie, she ate what Gunnar ordered for her, and obediently walked along the trails he chose. And she silently hugged and loved on a slightly shaken Willow at every opportunity.

Finally at night, after the tuckered-out child was fast asleep from hiking the trails near Old Faithful, Gunnar and Kat sat outside their log cabin in two rustic chairs—a chilled bottle of Riesling between them.

"His death was a shock, though he's been dead to me for half my life or longer. To think he's been alive and a father to someone else, is hard to fathom. What really hurts is that he stayed for her, and not for me," she said simply. "My dad didn't abandon Sassy or her mom… and I'm jealous of that. It makes me feel… *lesser than.*"

"Lesser than what?" Gunnar asked, softly.

"Lesser than *her*. Like I wasn't as good, or as pretty, or as valued by him."

Gunnar swallowed hard and reached over for her hand. It was cold and lifeless, but he held on tight for the both of them until at last, she grabbed hold and met his eyes. Both had unshed tears leaning in towards each other.

"You scared us, Kat," Gunnar choked out, "Willow and me. Please promise me you'll never leave. That you'll come and find me instead."

She nodded.

"I'm so ashamed of myself for frightening you both. It was just a blind impulse that I couldn't control. I know it's because I let dark thoughts take hold, so it's on me. I wonder if that's how my dad felt when he left... maybe we're more alike than I thought, him and me."

Gunnar frowned and shook his head at her words.

"Your dad shouldn't have left you. But he shouldn't have left Sassy, either. Two wrongs definitely do not make a right."

Kat regarded his words as she took a sip of her cold wine.

"I know," she whispered.

"I like Sassy," Gunnar said carefully, "and I think you would too, if you gave her a chance. She's not the one who hurt you, Kat. She's not your dad."

"But..." Kat agonized over her answer. "...she looks like him."

Gunnar nodded.

"Again, not her fault. For the record, I think she looks like you. Like a *lesser-than* version of Kat West, without the trademark Kat West command of the world around her."

"Give her time," Kat replied under her breath.

Kat was smiling, and nearly laughing at Gunnar's observations.

"Nah—she'll always be the deputy," he said, "never the Sheriff."

That did it. Kat let out a laugh that allowed the tears to fall, breaking whatever spell held Kat at such a low point.

"What do you say, Sheriff," he said, gently taking the glass from her shaking hand. "Should we call it a night?"

"You might have to carry me, I'm so tired," she said with a sniffle as she brushed her lips against his. Her chestnut hair fell in waves against his bare forearms like an unraveling bolt of silk, sending shockwaves through his body. As she kissed him, Kat slid a warm hand under the collar of his shirt, caressing his neck. Hungry for her touch, Gunnar lifted his shoulder to trap her hand, willing it to stay.

"Oh," he said as he stood up and lifted her in his arms, "I can do that, Mrs. West."

CHAPTER 45

"So, you're saying car engineers don't work at all in the summer?"

Freda was sitting next to Erik at Red's BBQ, at an outdoor picnic table overlooking the river. Erik had his body slightly turned towards Freda, silently communicating his interest in the pretty girl, who wore a coral-colored dress and strappy sandals.

Her tawny skin glowed, Ash thought, thanks to a little makeup. He'd known Freda for years and always assumed she was a confirmed tomboy.

"Just like your livestock," Erik said, "car design, manufacturing and sales have cycles. Things happen in summer, but not much. Everyone is focused on selling the newest models. Come fall, it'll be back to the drawing board."

"Ash confessed it was hard to leave Lake Michigan after school," Freda said.

"I thought he was nuts to go," Erik replied, "until I got here. Seeing Wyoming for myself, why, now I'm questioning everything. Why am I an engineer? Why can't I be a cowboy—or should I say, *caint?*"

Everyone laughed as Red himself delivered their dinner, one tasty dish after another.

"Howdy all," he bellowed to the welcoming group. "Jackie and I are looking forward to coming to West Ranch tomorrow, as guests. Now boys, don't go hogging all the pretty girls at the dance. My nephew, Wayne, has got to have a fightin' chance, too."

"Heard and understood, Red," Ash said. "I'm one of the hosts, so I have to make sure everyone has a good time. I'll look out for Wayne."

"We all will," Freda chimed in. "Wayne's a good egg. I'll be sure to give him a dance. Just tell him to leave his muddy ranching boots at home. I know where they've been."

After dinner, with Sassy sitting by his side and Freda and Erik in the back seat of the open Jeep, Ash drove towards the walking path that wound along the gorge. The sun was setting, and he hoped that if Erik and Freda walked ahead a little, he might get in a kiss or two from Sassy. He reached over and took her hand.

"You look pretty tonight," he said, as low as he could get away with and still be heard. Not that it mattered much; the two in the back were laughing and talking against the rush of the wind around them, not giving a thought to anyone else.

Sassy was wearing a simple black dress made of a gauzy fabric that hugged her in all the right places. Her boots were shining with fresh leather polish, and turquoise and sterling earrings set off her tanned skin and buttery golden hair. Sitting in the Jeep, the hemline of her dress rested on her thighs, revealing beautiful, sculpted limbs.

The breeze liked to catch her flouncy hem, teasing him with tantalizing glimpses.

Ash tried to forget lying next to Sassy on a picnic blanket as he kissed her at length. How his hand moved from her hipbone to her shoulder, and then her back. Her one simple touch—as her finger gently brushed the exposed skin by his snap buttons—sent him reeling.

He pushed away the memories of holding her close in the dark of the ranch house, kissing her harder and more passionately than he'd ever done in his life, and wanting more.

The growing attraction was dangerous, and he was playing with fire. A girl like Sassy would never stay where a man wanted her to; she would do the leading. All the way back to Illinois, most likely, and her only family. The odds of Sassy staying in Wyoming after her summer internship were slim to none. If he continued to open himself to her, he'd be dropped like a hot rock come September, leaving his heart shattered.

Better to cut his losses now, while he was merely smitten. Rather than later, when he was full-blown head over heels in love.

Right?

His resolve weakened as the two walked along the moonlit path by the gorge, easily holding hands. Freda and Erik had dashed ahead, in a hurry to spot wildlife in the tall bushes.

"You are quiet tonight," Sassy whispered, her head momentarily resting on Ash's shoulder. "What's on your mind?"

Ash smiled sadly in the dark.

"You," he said. "Us. What's to become of us."

"Do you really need to have all the answers, Ash?"

"Not all, but some of the answers. How about just one answer. Like, *where*? Where will you be at the end of summer? I've decided that my future is at West Ranch. But as Erik said at dinner, now I'm questioning everything."

Sassy stopped walking, and turned to face Ash.

"Erik was making a joke, Ash, and you're not. Nobody knows what's ahead. I didn't know my father was going to die so young, or that I'd end up here, in West Gorge. All the way from Illinois. I didn't know I'd meet you."

"But, what if…"

"Ash, you need to decide whether your future is a location or a person."

The comment confounded Ash for a moment, but then he answered.

"I want my future to have both. I want to live right here with someone I love. I want to be faithful; I want to correct the past. Build a family that knows its place in the world from the get-go; a family I can be true to." Ash paused to take a deep breath. "Is that so crazy?"

Looking into his eyes, Sassy knew that it was a lucky woman who would capture the heart of Ash West someday. She could see how vulnerable he was under the sculpted face, which most likely mirrored her own insecurities. She wouldn't toy with him.

Dropping his hand, she answered.

"It's not crazy, Ash. It's beautiful. But if living in Wyoming is on the top of your list, then maybe we should just be friends. That's a big *ask* and I'm not ready to commit to anything, anyone, or any place—I know you're not asking me to, right? We only just noticed each other. Just got our diplomas, and all. I'm not sure what I want for dinner tomorrow, let alone where I want to live."

Ash's throat tightened up. He began to reach for her, but his arms froze midway to their destination, and dropped again. She looked sad, and he could see the last of the setting sun reflect upon Sassy's shining hair and glowing skin. When she blinked, a lone tear escaped down her cheek, and he was helpless to wipe it away. He knew that if he touched her even once, he'd be a goner.

"Sassy, I..." Ash began in a hoarse whisper.

"*Guys!* You'll never guess what we saw."

Erik and Freda came running back, laughing and talking over each other, and oblivious to Ash and Sassy's painful exchange.

"What an amazing first day in Wyoming," Erik exclaimed as the foursome walked to the Jeep. "I can't wait for tomorrow."

"Yee haw," Ash mumbled darkly under his breath, sadly making his way to the Jeep.

CHAPTER 46

The morning of the West Ranch cookout started out with a sprinkle of rain, but winds from the West blew out the clouds, leaving blue skies and sunshine. In the early morning light, teams of vendors descended on West land. They knew it would take all-hands on deck to be ready for the afternoon event—the biggest social event of year.

Under the tent, erected the day before, tables and chairs lined up in proximity to the half-dozen food trucks the Wests hired for the party. Guest could have their choice of BBQ, burgers, tacos, or wood-fired pizzas made to order—or all of the above.

"And y'all save room," someone would inevitably shout, for cupcakes and ice cream sundaes.

Using the West's soaring lodge pole pine pavilion as the hub of the wheel, a coordinator with a clipboard and headset directed the assembly of a dance floor adjacent to a portable band shell. Hay bales were dropped in a circle around an iron bonfire pit. And a shaded area under a large tree provided the older guests a spot to sit and gossip, away from the music.

The younger guests weren't forgotten. There were water games, hay rides and bounce houses, and a few dozen floating toys in the stream, tethered to the shore. A miniature "road" was constructed, complete with traffic signs and accompanied by child-sized ATVs, scooters and bikes.

At Kat's insistence, the event planner hired a dozen young life-guards and camp counselors from town to oversee the safety of the children, and a registered nurse to man a first aid station. This was after her own first attendance had been punctuated by bandaging scraped knees, fetching water bottles to cure dehydration, and dispensing antacids.

Where's that doctor—where's Kat?

She was beckoned all day long, in between bites of her BBQ sand-wich and talking with people from other ranches. One guest even asked her to take a look at a skin tag that had been bothering her for months.

"Now I see why you wanted a doctor in the family," she dead-panned to Gunnar as she fell into bed at the end of that exhausting day.

Gunnar had called Ash as he was leaving town a few days before, and apologized for not being home when Erik Olsen arrived for a visit. "I can't say much right now," he told the boy. "Getting Kat out of town for a few days is important. I'll explain when I can."

"Will you be back for the cookout?" Ash asked.

"I'm not sure," Gunnar said, "that's up to my wife."

Their trip was a mystery to Ash, and unsettling—selfishly, he could use his brother's advice. But judging from the tone in Gunnar's voice, he had his own problems to sort out. Since arriving back home, Ash had been getting a taste of the power and complexities a beautiful woman could bring into a man's life.

Just a boy at the time, he'd had a front row seat to Kat and Gunnar's love story when they were all quarantined at the hospital years before. Now, Gunnar's devotion to his wife was undeniable. But wasn't he just as devoted to West Ranch? Would he move away if Kat asked him to?

Pike left the ranch to pursue his art, but remained in West Gorge. Colton left the ranch operation to build a construction company in town. Even Ridge walked away from the day-to-day chores—first in his depression, and then in his happiness and desire to be with Casey.

They were different; their identities were firmly rooted in the land and the people around them, and though nobody made him feel that way, Ash was a latecomer.

"You have a seat at the table," Ridge told him when the adoption was finalized, "same as the rest of us. A full portion of the good, the bad, and the ugly that is West Ranch."

Ridge had been modest; there was no bad or ugly that Ash could detect.

An attorney went over the trusts and inheritance set up in his name, and indeed, his portion was staggeringly full—mind-blowing, in fact. More money than he knew a fellow could have at his fingertips. He thought the money his granny left him upon her death was a windfall, but it couldn't hold a candle to the West money.

"What do I have to do in return?" Ash had asked the attorney, wondering what the catch was; what strings might be attached. But the lawyer had smiled kindly.

"Just be Ash West," he said.

Ridge and his new brothers gave him the absolution and fresh start he craved. A chance to lay down his anger and his thieving ways. *Acting out,* the therapist called his behavior; *stealing,* Officer Jason Scott had called it. They were both right. But as a West, Ash could move forward in life with a safety net of love, forgiveness, and the means to build a bright future.

Ash knew he couldn't earn what he'd been handed, but that didn't make him long any less to earn it. He wanted more than anything to be a match for it, at any rate, by pouring himself into the ranch business with a heart of gratitude. And to do that, he needed to be front and center in West Gorge, Wyoming.

In the morning light, the sweetness of his homecoming was nothing but a bitter taste in his mouth. The woman he was falling in love with told him to move along if he wanted a commitment from her. Ash should have backed off. He should have let his frustration with Sassy breathe before taking his next steps.

But he didn't. He sent a text instead that he deeply regretted, asking Amber to be his date for the big ranch cookout.

"Why, I'd love to," she'd answered quickly, sealing the deal.

Now he was dreading the event that he'd been talking up to his friend Erik. His heart felt painfully squeezed by some unknown force, and he just wanted to talk with Sassy and work things out. At the same time, he felt guilty for giving Amber the wrong idea about his intentions, which were nothing but friendly.

Why did he have to agonize about Sassy's long-term plans? Why had he told Amber the cookout was a date?

"Just be Ash West" hadn't served him well in the past few days, trying to navigate his love life with zero experience.

"Just be Ash West" was a clumsy idiot.

CHAPTER 47

"Welcome, everyone," Ridge said easily into the microphone. He paused to give guests by the hundreds time to stop their conversations and turn his way. A few old cowboys were in the middle of shaggy dog stories, and were not going down without a fight.

"I remember the year my mom and daddy first hosted a West Ranch cookout—about two dozen folks came from town and surrounding ranches. Now, look at us all!"

Hoots and applause broke out in all the groups.

"I'm going to let you get back to your dancing and gabbing and eatin', but I want to give you a few ground rules. First, pick up after yourself—I ain't your nanny."

The crowd laughed heartily at Ridge's comment.

"Second, keep your talk clean. My grandbabies are running around."

Many women nodded in appreciation.

"And last, no fistfights over politics or religion. I'm looking at you, Marta."

At that, everyone laughed and applauded, while Marta Scott laughed the loudest.

"Now, have fun," Ridge said. "Oh, and one last comment for the church ladies. I'm not a young man; I'm only dancing with my wife tonight. Now let's party!"

Ridge handed the microphone back to the event planner and reached out for Casey's hand as the band struck up a song. Together, the two made their way to the parquet dance floor by the river, where she fell into his arms as he spun her around. Soon, others were following suit.

"Ridge West," Casey said with a mischievous smile as they swayed back and forth, "I could tell those church ladies a thing or two that would make them blush, and make you out to be a liar—not a young man, my foot. Why, just last night…"

"Oh, you don't want to go and do that." Ridge pulled her closer and whispered roughly in her ear. "It took me years to get them off my scent. Look at the lengths I had to go to, marrying you and all."

Casey gave him a playful swat on the backside of his jeans.

"You must have thought you were doing me a favor," she teased, "marrying the old maid realtor."

"Casey girl, everyone knows you got the short end of the stick with this marriage," Ridge said with a wicked smile of his own, "but I'm going to hold you to it."

Before Casey could comment, Ridge kissed her hard on the lips, and then swung her into a dip before twirling her again. Off to one side of the dance floor, a group of elderly women from the Presbyterian sewing circle sat eating tacos and drinking lemonade.

"He doesn't look that old to me," one mumbled in complaint, as the others agreed.

"Or tired!"

CHAPTER 48

*S*assy sat on a haybale off to the sidelines—her self-imposed normal. She was used to laying low at obligatory gatherings, and avoiding the ones she could.

"Why bring attention to myself," she'd say to her perplexed parents by way of explanation.

"Why sit at home instead of enjoying life?" Her mother would counter.

She was beginning to think there was a grain of truth to what her mother said. Maybe she had sat at home too much, out of the fear of standing out. Maybe there was such a thing as being too comfortable with being anonymous. She'd missed out on a lot.

But getting involved with Ash was a miscalculation.

An *overcorrection.*

Initially, she thought he was a means to an end... a way into the front door of West Ranch, and a conversation with the family. Thanks to Gunnar, she could check that off her list and move to the next step. So, the boy wasn't necessary.

"But he's gorgeous, and he makes me feel... what?" Sassy mumbled to herself as she watched him on the dance floor with Amber. "He makes me *feel.*"

Amber, Sassy assumed, was gloating at the turn of events and unexpected invitation. Watching the girl arrive with Ash, getting out of his Jeep like Cinderella at the ball, felt like a dagger twisting in Sassy's flesh. She wanted to run far and fast, but stupidly, she'd caught a ride to the party with Freda and Eric. Nobody would be heading back to town for hours.

Ash wore a faded denim shirt that looked spray-painted onto his torso. With the pearl snaps undone at the cuffs and his sleeves rolled up, Sassy could see the tanned arms that just about drove her crazy. Those arms had pulled her close for more than one lingering kiss. She'd caressed them, marveling at how capably they wrapped around her, yet how gently they brushed stray curls from her face.

Sassy felt sick to her stomach watching those same arms hold Amber, and she wanted to cry. But under that denim shirt of Ash's beat a stubborn heart; a heart too set in its ways for such a young man.

"I just needed more time, Ash," Sassy said miserably, under her breath, "to give you the answers you're looking for."

The answers Amber already has, no doubt.

She forced herself to look away, and caught Freda smiling and dancing with Erik Olsen and having a great time. It should have been she and Ash. Would have been, but for the things weighing them down—his crazy expectations, and her bombshell of a secret.

So instead of spending the day anticipating a moonlight dance with Ash West, Sassy poured her energy into helping Freda get ready for the party. They chose the perfect dress, then Sassy meticulously blew out Freda's damp hair with a dryer and brush so her butter-scotch highlights would swing with life as Erik turned her this way and that.

The efforts paid off. Freda was the prettiest girl at the party, and Sassy tried to let that be satisfaction enough—it might have been, but for the pain of watching Ash with his date.

Sassy brushed a tear off her cheek, and wondered if this was how it was supposed to be. Maybe Ash was meant to be with Amber after college, and she had only upset the apple cart when she arrived at the ranch, like a time traveler who steps on a tiny ant and throws history out of whack forever.

But things were being set to rights now, Sassy thought, as she watched Amber in her cowboy's arms. Order was being restored. Because she was always going to leave Wyoming at the summer's end... wasn't she?

"Care to dance?" Looking up, she saw one of the young ranch hands, Wayne, standing next to her with his hand outstretched. Sassy wanted to say no, but appreciated the courage it took to approach her this way.

"Yes, thank you Wayne," Sassy said as she stood. The band began playing a boot-scootin' boogie number that kept them dancing apart, to Sassy's relief. She smiled at Wayne and put some unfelt energy into pretending to have fun.

It was almost fun, dancing under the star-filled Wyoming sky on a balmy summer night. When the song stopped, the dancers applauded the band and waited for the next number. Sassy wondered if it was too soon to excuse herself, but the bandleader spoke.

"We're going to slow things down for all you sweethearts out there," he said with the first notes of what could only be a romantic tune about moonlight and fireflies. Sassy cringed inside and was about to beg off when a man's hand appeared on Wayne's shoulder.

"Mind if I cut in, man?" Ash offered a handshake to her dance partner.

Wayne tipped his hat to Sassy, and she nodded with a weak smile. Heart hurting at the sight of Ash West, she took a step backwards, away from him. But he reached out and gently pulled her towards him.

"Please dance with me, Sassy," Ash whispered when she resisted.

Not wanting to embarrass him at his family's party or make a scene, Sassy slowly walked into Ash's arms, placing her hands loosely and reluctantly on his broad shoulders.

Ash wasn't having any of her reticence.

He reached up and took one of her limp hands in his own, and tucked it tight against his chest. Then he took his other hand and wrapped his arm around her waist, pulling her close.

Sassy frowned. It was what she wanted, but not like this.

"Ash... I..."

She stiffened as he drew her body towards his own, but it was in vain. The warmth radiating from his hands and body melted her. Sassy's broken heart raced as she turned her head to look over his shoulder.

Don't look in his eyes, she told herself. *And do not cry.*

"Sass..." Ash moaned miserably into her hair, burying his face. "I'm so sorry. I shouldn't have pressed you so hard, or demanded answers from you. I had no right."

He squeezed her hard and she felt as though he was squeezing unbidden tears to roll down her face. Sassy's throat felt hot and dry, with a painful lump where her words were supposed to be.

"Can you forgive me, Sass?"

Turning just a bit towards him, she was hit with the musky scent of the bare skin on his neck, and in spite of the way it surprised her, it smelled like home. Wherever that scent was, and the heat and strength from those arms, that's where Sassy wanted to be.

The tears pooling in her eyes were hot, and were about to fall, right there in front of God, the Wests and everybody—at a party where others were laughing and having a great old time. She had no choice but to bury her face in Ash's collar to hide her emotions. He must have felt her tears and her quivering because he held on tight and pulled her closer, dancing her slowly to a dark corner of the parquet floor and away from view.

"Shh, it's okay," he crooned as he gently kissed the side of her face.

Sassy sobbed.

She cried out of relief to be back in Ash's arms, though the same obstacles remained. She cried out of sadness at losing her father, and because the weight of the secret he'd saddled her with was too great. She cried at Kat's coldness towards her, and at her mother's shallow grief—Sugar's heart should be shattered at the loss of Jack. And Sassy cried at the thought of returning home, only to find *home* to be a cold apartment. Her own childhood house likely sold and demolished.

She never felt so alone. Sassy wanted Ash to kiss her; kiss the hurts away forever and never stop. But was this a pity dance? Was he simply being a good host, making sure everyone had a good time?

Minutes later, after two more slow songs, Sassy was finally able to breathe deeply and get her emotions in check. Pulling her face from Ash's neck, she got the courage to look into his eyes and tell him the thing that lay like a stone between them.

"Ash," she began quietly, "there's something you ought to know."

But before she could say any more, Freda's surprised voice cut across the dance floor and stopped her cold.

"*James Timothy*," Freda exclaimed. "What the *hey howdy* are you doing here?"

CHAPTER 49

"*I* could ask you the same thing," Freda's long-time boyfriend said mildly. The young people had all moved off of the dance floor and formed a circle—Ash to support Erik and prevent any loud argument, and Sassy, who felt she should stay close to Freda until further notice.

"When you didn't come home this weekend or answer my calls, I came to see if you were okay," James Timothy said evenly. "But I see you're just fine tonight, Freda." His eyes softened as he gazed at her admiringly. "*So* fine. Beautiful, in fact."

Freda swallowed hard.

"Looks like you're having fun and I'm glad," James Timothy said, looking around and acknowledging the little group. "I haven't been a lot of fun this summer, what with studying for the bar, and sending out resumes. Becoming a lawyer is one thing, but accepting the right first job is another. This decision will determine the trajectory of my career, and my ability to take care of my... *family*... if I'm blessed with one, someday."

James Timothy reached for Freda's hand when he said this, but lost his confidence and dropped it again, looking at her with all the love and longing of a homesick puppy, Sassy thought.

"I feel ya, man," Erik said to him.

Freda sighed heavily and turned to Erik.

"James Timothy, this is Erik Olsen, Ash West's friend from Michigan. We've been showing him around West Gorge." James Timothy shook hands with Erik, and then Ash and Sassy as Freda continued the introductions.

"How do you do," he said to everyone. "I've heard a lot about y'all, especially you, Sassy. Freda tells me what a good friend you've become."

Sassy smiled. She couldn't help but like the tall, handsome Jim Tim, who only had eyes for Freda Lang. With his humble, unassuming mannerisms, it was hard to see him as the villain Freda painted him out to be. Sassy thought him a perfectly grounded counterpoint to her more spirited friend.

"Hey, I see someone I know," the unflappable Erik said to a surprised group. "Excuse me."

Ash and Sassy watched as Erik walked over to Amber and asked her to dance. Moments later, the two were smiling and laughing on the parquet floor while Freda had quietly slipped her hand into James Timothy's own.

Sassy imagined it fit like a glove.

"Sorry I've been so aloof these past few weeks, Freda. You deserve so much better. I'll go back home if you want, but... well, you know I've loved you since I was fifteen. You're the motivation behind every-thing I do. I only want to work hard and be worthy of you."

Bolstered by her simple gesture, he reached up and took a few strands of her hair and tucked it behind her ear. Then he let his thumb gently travel down her jawline. The touch was so intimate, Sassy thought she should look away.

"Have you eaten?" Freda asked tenderly as she stepped closer to her beau, leading him to the food trucks.

After Freda and James Timothy were out of earshot, Sassy looked up at Ash, who had been holding her hand, and the two broke into laughter.

"Did that just really happen?" Sassy asked through her smile.

"See, Wyoming has everything you could want, Sassy," Ash said through his own smile, while reaching up and brushing away an undried tear from her face, "dancing and drama..."

"Jealousy and intrigue..." she added.

"And tacos... did I mention tacos?"

He leaned over and kissed her cheek.

"Have *you* eaten?" Sassy asked, taking Ash's arm and walking towards the food. "You know how punchy you get, and how bad your jokes get when you're tired and hungry."

"Then let's go eat," he said, putting his arm around Sassy. "You can finish telling me what you started to say on the dance floor. Something I should know?"

"Oh yeah, that..." Sassy took a deep breath, summoning the courage to tell Ash her secret. She was saved by a sweet little voice.

"Uncle Ash! Uncle Ash," Willow West came running up with Sun and Ford close behind. "I'm back from Yellowstone, Uncle Ash," she said, "and I can't wait to tell you about the geysers and the bison. And we saw a bear!"

"A bear," little Ford echoed in awe.

"Wow!" Ash bent down to be closer to the three children in front of him. I can't wait to hear all about it, but it might have to wait until tomorrow. You see, I'm as hungry as a bear," he said, with a theatrical raising of his "claws" and a *roar*.

The kids all laughed with glee and ran away in pretend fear. When Ash and Sassy looked up again, Kat West was standing in front of them, staring at Sassy.

"Hey Kat," Ash said tentatively, unable to gauge Kat's mood.

"Ash," she said with a cool nod. "Gunnar is by the taco truck, looking for you. If you don't mind, I'd like to speak with Sassy for a minute."

Ash looked at Sassy as though he didn't want to let go of her hand. He felt protective, and something definitely seemed off, but he didn't know what.

"It's okay," Sassy smiled up at him. "I'll catch up with you in a few minutes."

He looked at Kat again and then gave Sassy a kiss on the cheek before wandering away.

The two women sized each other up silently. Each with their invisible shield and armor, protecting themselves from the pain they knew each other could cause.

Sassy fully expected Kat to raise a pointed finger and send her away at any moment; she pictured two cowboy body guards with guns in their holsters taking her by the arms, and carrying her out of West Ranch forever—barring her from re-entry.

Instead, Sassy watched Kat's steely appraisal of her slowly go from anger and denial to self-preservation, then to curiosity. Maybe even compassion. When at last she detected a slight softening in Kat's eyes, Sassy spoke.

"You *know* who I am, don't you?"

Kat was silent.

"I'm your sister, Kat."

CHAPTER 50

"*H*alf."

Sassy studied Kat's face in the light coming off the dance floor. The two stood near a tall pine tree, in relative privacy considering the hundreds of party guests dancing, laughing and eating in the vicinity.

The younger girl had no idea how the older had discovered the truth, but judging from the look on her face, there was no doubt she'd somehow put the pieces together.

"You're my *half*-sister," Kat said, as Sassy stood mutely in front of her.

Sassy's face broke into a tired laugh at the unkind comment.

This was not her first encounter with Kat West, but the first time they faced each other as equals. Sassy felt relief wash over her that the truth was out, knowing she was close to being done with her father's thankless task. Soon, she could walk away from Kat, and West Gorge, forever.

"Whatever gets you through the night, sister," Sassy remarked, "or *half*-sister… I don't care. I don't have a horse in this race, Kat. I'm just Jack's messenger."

Kat's mouth squeezed tight, tersely, Sassy observed. Her big-bad-wolf of a half-sister didn't enjoy not being in control, she could see.

"So, what's Jack's message, Sassy?"

Me. I'm the message.

Sassy had a sudden urge to shake Kat by the shoulders and wake her up to the realization that they were blood relatives—kin, in a nearly kinless world. Kat was surrounded by Wests, but her only blood family was her mother, her daughter, and now a sister. Half-sister. Wasn't something so rare worth nurturing and protecting?

Give her more time, she thought. The same thing she herself had wanted from Ash.

"I couldn't tell you what his message is, Kat," Sassy said at last. "He gave me a package for you, but obviously I don't have it with me."

Kat considered this and nodded.

Sassy watched with interest as Kat's face reflected the battle warring within her. The hard shell wasn't sustainable, and eventually melted into a softer expression, with glimmers of both hope and hopelessness. Sassy felt compassion and pity for the abandoned child Kat used to be, and the conflicted adult she'd become.

"Sassy..." Kat said tentatively, "I know I can be... I haven't made this easy for you, I know. I'm trying to remember that you are not the one I'm mad at. You're not my enemy."

Haltingly, Kat lifted her arm up, and Sassy felt a childlike happiness that her sister wanted to take her hand. But just as quickly, she saw that Kat was handing her a small card.

Taking it, she smirked and gave her head a slight shake at Kat's tough exterior.

Can I ever break through?

CHAPTER 51

"Oh look, Kat and Gunnar are back," Liu was on the dance floor with her arms wrapped around Colton's shoulders. Colton nodded and caught the attention of Pike and Paislee who were dancing nearby, and gestured to where Kat stood, talking to Sassy.

"Something's going on," Colton said to his wife, looking into her eyes and pulling her closer—which wasn't easy. The baby was growing bigger each day.

"Yes, I agree," Liu said with a smile at the feeling of Colton's strong arms around her. "As my grandmother says, *yǒuyuán qiānlǐ lái xiānghuì,* fate brings people together from far apart."

"You're so beautiful—so *měi lì* when you speak Chinese," Colton said with a slight bow before spinning his wife around with the song. As she laughed, he reached close to nuzzle her soft neck and sleek hair. The hand that sat on her back gently caressed the smooth dress that fit her like a second skin.

"Ah, you've been listening in on my language lessons to the children," Liu teased.

"*Shi,*" Colton answered.

Liu held his gaze, though it was still counter-intuitive to the way she was raised. Looking into her husband's eyes, she felt a warmth spread throughout her body as she pressed closer to him. She loved the sound of this boisterous, playful man as he boldly attempted to speak the melodic language of her childhood.

Colton, she believed, had been underestimated his entire life by nearly everyone, and nearly by her. But this former athlete and joke-ster had hidden depths, and dreams that came to life when they met; dreams that deepened after he left the ranch and began his own building company.

Their own home, impressive in scale, was a masterpiece of thoughtful details—a love song to both Liu's exotic heritage and contemporary sensibilities. Colton tirelessly designed and built a home with his wife's extended family in mind, and her love for cooking.

In the mornings, Liu lovingly planted, watered and harvested her kitchen garden, bringing in great armfuls of flowers to put in the jade and ironstone vases. In the afternoons, Colton could find Liu sitting back in the tea house he built for her, adjacent to the West River. There, the two would enjoy the wildlife and views of the gorge.

In the evenings, Liu would invite her husband to *Zuòzhe chī,* sit and eat. She nourished his body and soul with fresh dishes, gentle shoulder massages, and stories from her day.

If her parents and grandparents had any reservations about their marriage, they were quickly dispelled. Colton welcomed them fully into their lives. He even designed a custom home with passage to their own. Before long, Zhang and Ling, and the elder Chun and Tao, had been installed as full-time residents. Each a willing babysitter for Sun, Ford, or Willow, and each one eagerly awaiting the arrival of Liu and Colton's baby.

But for now, the Chens were on an extended visit with family in China, and Liu was enjoying the calm before the excitement that her baby's arrival would bring.

And without their watchful eyes, Liu felt free to be more *American* with her demonstrations of love, openly caressing her husband's shoulders, and stealing a kiss or two under the moonlight.

The dress she slipped on for the party had been no accident. It felt like a second skin, and she knew Colton would be delighted with the velvety texture. He was a simple man who only desired the affections of his wife.

NEARBY, PAISLEE WEST ENJOYED FEELING PIKE'S HANDS ON HER WAIST as they danced and twirled under the stars. Her sleeveless dress had a romantic ruffle reminiscent of the prairie, which, she knew, sparked her husband's imagination.

Though it was full-on summer, they were both easily reminded of the days spent together as strangers, snowed in at a settler's cabin at the edge of the West property. She had gone in search of him and the answers she thought he might have to long-buried family secrets.

A blizzard on her heels, Paislee was rescued by Pike, who nurtured and cared for her.

Nobody knew where she was, including her then fiancée. And it didn't take long to fall head over heels in love with Pike West—who was miserably in love with Paislee, knowing there was another man in her life.

Five years later, they shared a spectacular modern farmhouse in West Gorge, a love of fine art, and two beautiful children, Sun and Ford.

Paislee looked up at the tall, trim Pike and flashed a dazzling smile. He was a quiet man whose still waters ran deep. She never knew if he was plotting his next painting or thinking about her, but Paislee allowed him his introspection—he shared when he was ready. And she was always pleased.

If she asked him, he might say, "both, as a matter of fact. I was thinking I might want *you* to sit for my next painting. Would you?"

Of course, she'd answer. She would do anything for her husband, the man who would give her any life she desired. As an heiress to a large fortune, there wasn't anything she couldn't buy—except the love of Pike West. That love was an amazing gift that she protected more than her family's most guarded treasures.

"Pike," she asked as he held her close, "what do you make of that Sassy from the ranch office? What's going on with her and Kat?"

Pike was quiet as he gazed in their direction.

"Time will tell," he said. "All I can say is that Kat hasn't smiled much this summer, and I suspect Sassy has something to do with that. That and the hasty trip Gunnar took her on."

It was Paislee's time to be silent. She pulled closer to Pike to ward off the ghost of family and marriage troubles, lest they be contagious. As if he understood, Pike tightened his hold on his wife and kissed the side of her cheek.

"Now don't be borrowing trouble, Mrs. West," he said into her ear, causing her to shudder from deep within. "You and I have nothing to fear or worry about, do we?"

"*Oh,*" Paislee whispered back in his ear, as her body flinched slightly at the unexpected pleasure of his rumbling voice. "I suppose we don't."

Pike flashed her a private smile, then buried his face in the thick waves of her hair.

$\mathscr{N}$umber 22 was easy to find in the high-end West Gorge condo complex, but Sassy had a hard time bringing herself to knock on the door. Her hands were sweaty and she fumbled the package in her hand several times.

"Come to my condo for lunch on Tuesday," Kat said at the cookout before walking away. It was an order, not an invitation.

"If Gunnar and Rowdy will let me leave work…" Sassy attempted.

"They will." Kat said simply, after handing Sassy a card with the address.

Of course they will, Sassy thought.

All that morning and the entire day before, Gunnar and Rowdy had been acting strangely. They weren't cold or distant, just the opposite. They were looking at her through a new lens, she thought. Sassy also detected a note of pity, as they must know that she was heading into the lion's den, and that Kat West was a formidable opponent when crossed.

If two strapping cowboys were shaking in their leather boots, then what chance did little Sassy Tate stand against her?

Ash didn't know anything yet, she could tell.

Sassy lost her nerve and never did tell Ash the secret she brought with her to Wyoming. The moment came and went. She decided that she would stay small and invisible in the interim, to save her strength for her meeting with Kat. Sassy was cool to Ash, turning down invitations to go on plum ranch assignments, or out to dinner. At home, she ate her dinner in silence then retreated to her room.

"I'm just tired, Freda," she told her roomie. "Let me rest up and then I want to hear everything about you and *Jim*... I mean, James Timothy Freemont."

Freda smiled indulgently. Usually so in tune with Sassy, probing into her every mood, the Lander girl was preoccupied with being reunited with her beau, and making plans for their future together.

Monday afternoon, the girls had rallied and said their farewells to Erik Olsen before the young engineer flew back to Detroit, and his awaiting job at General Motors.

"I'll never forget you two," Erik said generously, "or Wyoming. This visit was epic."

"Epic," the girls said in unison, and everyone laughed. Ash eyed her longingly, hoping, no doubt, for a private moment with her to find out what had been preoccupying her lately. But Sassy was only focused on her meeting with Kat, and would not be diverted by Ash.

Now, here she was—wondering what Kat's demeanor would be like today.

Kat opened right away after Sassy rang the doorbell of the condo, and motioned for her to enter. Sassy marveled that her sister owned this luxurious apartment, as well as the large house on the ranch.

"Hey," Kat said simply. She was barefoot, wearing jeans and a sweatshirt. Without makeup, and her hair pulled back at the nape of her neck, Kat didn't seem menacing at all—she almost seemed... approachable.

Using the spatula in her hand, she indicated the kitchen as she closed the door. "Nothing fancy. Grilled cheese sandwiches and potato chips."

"Comfort food," Sassy said without thinking, hoping she hadn't overstepped. It was a big deal that Kat had asked to meet, and she didn't want it to end too soon.

"Everyone needs a little comfort, I guess," Kat said with a shrug. "Grab the drinks, why don't you, and we'll take everything outside on the balcony. It's a pretty day."

Sassy followed Kat with the two iced teas and sat down at the table. The rushing waters of the West River provided ambient music in the background, accompanied by the beauty of the gorge, resplendent in mid-day shadows.

"You look just like him," Kat said before taking a bite.

"I've never heard that before," Sassy said. "I'm usually compared to my mother."

"It's in the eyes, and the stature," Kat said. "Your mother is... well?"

Sassy merely nodded. She understood how hard it was, how gracious it was, for Kat to ask this simple question.

"Your mother?"

Kat nodded back.

Sassy took a bite of her grilled cheese and waited for Kat to continue.

"So..." Kat ventured tentatively, "what did he tell you about me, before he died?"

After a lengthy exhale, Sassy answered. "That you existed, for starters. That he hadn't been in touch since he left you and your mother, but he knew where you lived. He told me about your career and achievements. Jack, my dad... *our dad*... wanted me to know that you were really smart as well as beautiful. So I could look up to you."

"Do you want money, is that why you came to the ranch?" Kat didn't sound accusing—she didn't need to. The words were accusing enough.

Sassy flinched as if slapped and her shoulders fell in defeat—they had a long way to go if this is what Kat thought. "No, I don't need money. Jack did all right." She didn't want to cry, but felt her lip trembling under the microscopic gaze of Kat. Of course that's what she'd think, marrying into such an immensely wealthy family. She hung her head to conceal her un-spilled tears.

Kat's hand reached across the table and covered her own shaking hand. When she looked back up, Sassy could see tears in Kat's eyes, too.

"I'm sorry, Sassy," Kat said. "That was crass and cold of me. I hate myself a little for asking that question."

"Kat, I don't need money, and I'm not here to mess up your life," Sassy managed to say, "or even be in your life. I'll probably pack up and leave after today. I've got a life to get back to, now that I've handled Jack's last wishes."

Kat shook her head sadly at the girl's words.

"Sassy Tate, I confess I just don't know how to act around you. I still can't get over the shock. You're so young and lovely. I look at you and see my own painful past, but also someone so familiar to me." Kat spoke as if she had a golf ball-sized lump in her throat. "I really did love him, you know. Even though we never understood each other. Even though he left. When you smile, I'm reminded of happier times that I'd pushed down and forgotten. And just maybe, that creates another type of hurt for me to feel. At all that he and I missed together."

"I guess Jack had a talent for messy exits," Sassy said.

Kat nodded.

"I see him in you too, Kat," Sassy said after a time. "The way you carry yourself, and speak as if the whole world is waiting for what you have to say."

"Don't tell my husband that, it will only confirm his suspicions."

Sassy smiled and relaxed a little. The sisters took a few bites of their sandwiches to allow their emotions to settle.

"Jack made me promise to come and find you," Sassy said. "Maybe he was afraid to do it himself after so much time, and rightly so. For the past year, I had to wrestle with his lies of omission along with his death. It's awful to grieve the loss of someone you love and be really mad at them at the same time. But I came to the conclusion that in spite of his failings, part of his legacy is the courage he gave me. And, I think, you."

As Kat silently regarded the words, Sassy reached into her purse and took out a small box, which she placed on the table.

"He asked me to give you this," Sassy told Kat, and then stood up to leave. "Do you mind if I... before I go... can I give you a small hug?"

Kat's eyes were fixated on the box, but when Sassy's words registered, she also stood and moved towards the girl, awkwardly at first.

Hugging Kat, Sassy thought, was like having a warm quilt hug her on a cold day. She breathed in the scent of her sister's hair and neck as Kat unintentionally rubbed Sassy's back like she was a child in need of reassurance. To Sassy, it felt like coming home, and tears filled her eyes again at the sensation.

Making herself break away, she turned to leave. Giving a small wave over her shoulder, she exited #22 and walked quickly to her car.

Sassy was spent. Driving the short distance to the bungalow was an effort, and she wanted nothing more than to curl up into a ball and cry with relief, in the privacy of her room. She had finally met with her sister—as sisters. And emotionally, she was dry. Physically, she could still feel the effects of Kat's arms around her, protecting and accepting her as she is, though tentatively.

But rest wouldn't come anytime soon, she could see. Ash was sitting on her front stoop, waiting for her. His jaw was tense as he eyed her warily, and his eyes were wide and a little wild, as if seeing her for the first time.

Walking as slowly as she could towards the house, Sassy avoided the inevitable until she was standing directly in front of Ash.

"You're Kat's sister!"

CHAPTER 53

"*Y*es, I am. I'm Kat's sister."

"That's why you came to West Ranch. To find her."

Sassy could only nod.

"You knew all along, but you didn't tell me."

"How could I tell you before I told Kat?"

"You didn't trust me."

"I hardly *knew* you."

Ash regarded her while he continued to piece together the events of the past few weeks.

"You used me to get to my family," he said, shaking his head in disbelief.

"I didn't..." Sassy began to protest, but knew he was right. Her shoulders slumped in defeat. "Everything I told you was true, Ash. I just left out my last name."

"So you're claiming a technicality? You deceived me, and I'm supposed to be okay because of a technicality?"

"I didn't deceive, exactly. I omitted."

As Sassy said this, she cringed with the realization that her father could claim the same thing, and it really didn't cut it.

She sat down on the stoop next to Ash, whose anger made him

rigid. There wasn't much room, but she squeezed in anyway, close to his leg and shoulder.

"Think about it Ash. Rowdy never would have hired me if he knew that I came to meet Kat. And Kat, tucked away in her *fortress*, wouldn't let me anywhere near her because of her anger towards Jack... our dad. I had to come and figure things out for myself."

Ash listened as Sassy continued.

"Tell me the truth," he said. "Were you using me?"

"At first," Sassy whispered.

Out of the corner of her eye, she saw Ash hang his head and drop his shoulders. He was hurting, but there was no stopping her now.

"After you started paying attention to me, I figured you were going to be my foot in the door," Sassy continued, "but then you got lodged somewhere between my heart and my head and messed everything up."

"Wait, *I* messed everything up?" Ash was angry, she knew.

"No, I did," she said. "I know I did. I messed up big time, stringing you along. You have every right to be mad."

"Gee Sassy, thanks for the validation."

"Stow the sarcasm, Ash. It's not a good look on you."

"Well, what do you suggest I do? How can I trust..."

"Stop, Ash. Stop right there." Sassy stood and faced Ash. When she spoke, there was an edge in her voice. "Thanks to my father, you're not the only one with trust issues. Yours and mine, they cancel each other out."

"Sassy, I..."

"And going forward, I suggest you do what I'm going to do—pretend none of this ever happened."

"That's your *plan*?"

"Yes, Ash. Finally, I'm revealing my master *plan*. I plan on going back home and pretending my dad didn't have another family."

And pretending I didn't fall in love with you, Ash.

She knew she handled the situation badly where Ash was concerned, yet an anger welled up inside her too—anger that Jack had put her in this situation. What was the right way to introduce yourself to a sister you never knew existed?

Sassy was angry that Ash couldn't see how hard it had all been for her—he couldn't see past his own pain to admit somebody else might be struggling, too.

"You're better off with Amber," Sassy said, her voice escalating in frustration. "She'll never leave you, and she'll never leave Wyoming. Check, and *check*—numbers one and two on Ash West's list of life goals."

"It's not like that. Amber is my friend," Ash protested.

"She wants to be more than a friend. Anyone can see that except you. Every time something doesn't go your way, you expect Amber to bolster your ego; to be someone you can bring around to make me jealous."

Sassy walked up the stairs and around Ash on her way to her front door, which she was about ready to slam and lock. Just as soon as she got in a parting shot.

"To lead Amber on is the same as me using you to get to Kat," Sassy said. "Think about that before you go placing yourself on a pedestal, Ash."

CHAPTER 54

*A*t #22, Kat glared at the package on the table for a long time, the one Sassy brought at their father's request. She'd been angry with him for most of her life, but now he was dead. What was the point in being angry with a dead man?

Giving her head a little shake, Kat reached across the table and drew it closer. It just fit inside her hand, and could be anything—a signed baseball, or a wad of money.

Open it, she told herself, but frowned at the thought. If she did, what would that mean? Did it mean that she was finally ready to forgive him and move on? Kat liked to control her own narrative, thank you very much, and discovering that she had a surprise sister, who traveled to Wyoming to deliver a surprise package, was two surprises too many.

But there the package sat.

"All right, Jack," Kat said out loud, tearing a tiny piece of the tape off the brown paper wrapper. "Let's see what you sent to make up for being a louse."

The box under the wrapping paper didn't give any additional clues.

When Kat took the lid off, she saw a folded envelope on top of a man's wristwatch. She set the envelope aside and took the watch out. It was Jack's all right, she'd know it anywhere. It had been a gift to Jack from her mother on the day Kat was born.

The inscription on the back read:

With Love, On Your First Father's Day

For years, Kat would bring it to her dad every morning as he got dressed for work, happy to breath in the steam emanating from the shower. It smelled of his spicy aftershave cologne. As she curled up under the unmade blankets, her father buttoned his starched shirt, threaded his cufflinks, and tied his tie.

"This here is a Windsor knot, kitty Kat," he'd tell her. "Over, around, down through the tunnel, and pull."

Some mornings he'd mix things us.

"I'm feeling lucky today, kitty Kat, let's do a double Windsor— around, *around*, over, down through the tunnel." For a brief moment, Kat wondered if her father wore a double Windsor the day Sassy's mother, Sugar, walked into the car dealership and stole him away. But Kat shook her head and the flash of anger dissipated.

After a spray of his cologne, Jack would slip on his wedding ring, and slide the watch onto his left wrist. He'd sit down by Kat then and patiently watch as she clasped the buckle with her pudgy baby hands.

"Well done, kitty Kat," he'd say, and give her cheek a kiss. "Now, what time is it?"

Together they'd look at his watch, and she'd answer.

"Time to go to work, Daddy."

Then one day, Kat remembered clearly, she no longer wanted to sit and watch the tie act, or help him with his watch. She was too cool, she thought; too old for the childish rituals, or being called *kitty Kat*.

"I'm just *Kat*," she snarked with an adolescent edge.

"Oh, okay," he said in surprise. The fact that he tried to hide his hurt at her snub was like a closed-fisted punch to her heart; one she could almost still feel. But if every irritable teenaged girl was found guilty and sentenced to abandonment by her parents, the world would be full of orphans, Kat knew.

She couldn't imagine Willow ever being so cold to Gunnar, but it was inevitable that they would face challenges. Thankfully, they had a ways to go.

Gingerly, she set the watch down and reached inside the envelope for the folded single sheet of paper, smoothing out the creases.

Kitty Kat, I am sorry for leaving you. More than you'll ever know. The worst thoughts you've had about me, all deserved, can't touch the way I've despised my actions – I was a different man while married to Trudy, but I should have been a better man for you, sweetheart. I can't give you back the time we lost but I never stopped loving you, or being proud of you. Your mother asked me to stay away and I respected that. She didn't want me to come in and out of your life, which is what I would have done. Upon reflection, here at the end of it all, I wish I'd fought harder for you, daughter. Kat, please be kind to your sister. I don't deserve this favor, but she does. She is innocent, same as you. One last thing. I set aside a sizable fund for your mother. My attorney will be contacting her to apprise her of this – it will allow her to retire in comfort. Ask her to not be too proud to accept it. I suspect you would not have wanted my money after all this time. You might have thought I was trying to buy your forgiveness. Forgive me, please, in your own time, but only for your sake. While my façade has been shiny and polished, my soul has been miserable and tormented. I wouldn't wish that on anyone, least of all my sweet and lovely Kitty Kat.

— Daddy

Daddy.

At seeing her father's handwriting and words after so many years,

181

Kat allowed herself to cry at all she'd lost. An old bitterness threatened to churn in her stomach again, until she remembered Gunnar's words ringing in her head.

"As an infectious disease doctor, you understand contagion, Kat," he said. "Hate and bitterness are as destructive as viruses, and they can do just as much damage."

He went on to say that he didn't want her to pass this sickness along to their marriage, and to their little daughter.

"Lay it down, Sheriff," Gunnar implored. "If it's bad blood, then let it go."

CHAPTER 55

*A*sh watched Sassy retreat to her little bungalow next door to his own. The way she closed the door left no doubt that he was not welcome to come in, or even to call her phone to continue their conversation. He would have to wait a few days.

Had he been wrong to accuse her so vehemently? He didn't think so. But driving back to the ranch, after his own anger and self-righteousness had cooled, Ash began to see things from Sassy's perspective.

"How could I tell you before I told Kat?"

Of course she'd been right about that. And maybe she was right about him being wrong, expecting her to be completely transparent from the get go—people needed time and space to unfold. He certainly did. Hardly anyone back at Michigan State University knew his deepest secrets and fears, or his insecurities.

Only Erik Olsen knew his history, which is why they were true friends. But Ash had not disclosed these things as freshman roomies, or sophomore frat brothers. Only going into their final year of school did Ash feel that Erik could be confided in.

But what about his own character?

"To lead Amber on, well it's wrong."

Sassy had been right about that, too. He had gone running to

Amber when things got tough. She was always glad to see him, and Amber did boost his confidence.

"And what do I do for Amber, except send her mixed signals?" Ash rebuked himself.

Back at the ranch office, Rowdy and Gunnar took him in wordlessly. They had told him about Sassy and Kat, thinking he had a right to know if he didn't already. Tightly wound secrets were unravelling fast, and they didn't want him to feel like a fool.

He took the news hard. And from the look on his face, Ash's encounter with Sassy only made things worse. Only time would tell where the dust would settle.

"I'm heading up by the pass," Ash scowled at the men, "to check on the new calves."

They could hear an ATV engine revving angrily, as gravel flew under tires during the impatient acceleration.

The next morning, Ash padded into the ranch house kitchen to find Ridge drinking his sunrise coffee.

"Thought I heard you come in," Ridge said. "Haven't seen you much these past weeks, what with you living in town. And your busy social calendar."

Ash nodded glumly as he poured his coffee and sat down with his dad.

"Sorry," Ash said.

"No need," Ridge chuckled, "it's healthy and normal for a boy your age to spend more time with young'uns than with your old man."

When Ash looked up, Ridge could see tears pooling in the boy's eyes, and he reached over to pull him in for a bear hug. Ash did not resist.

"I've messed everything up with Sassy. I fell for her… *hard*."

Ridge nodded and listened.

"I got scared, and I wanted her to commit to staying. She said it was too soon. Of course it was too soon," Ash moaned. "I'm such an idiot."

"Probably," Ridge said to his son's surprise. "Sassy had a lot going on this summer. More than you or I could ever guess." Ridge said slowly. "The girl deserved a healthy dose of grace, wouldn't you say?"

"Yes, but..."

"But nothing, Ash."

Ridge's tone was even, but there was no nonsense in it.

Ash scowled and pouted.

He thought for sure his dad would be on his side, and not Sassy's.

"Ash, you can't put conditions on love. You can't tell somebody you'll love them if they stay where you want. You just love 'em and work things out," Ridge said. "None of us knows the future. For all we know, Kat might get a chance to be a hospital director back in Chicago. She and Gunnar will cross that bridge if and when it comes. Paislee might want to live in Denver with her family, and she and Pike may or may not move. Casey has a family home in Phoenix, and I go with her because I love her."

"But... the ranch," Ash's justifications didn't have any momentum.

"Yes, it's a ranch. Not a prison," Ridge said.

CHAPTER 56

Sassy didn't show up for work the next day, or the next. Ash wanted to ask Freda where she was, but the girl wasn't giving off *approachable vibes*, he thought.

"Brrr, is it cold in here?" He mumbled when Freda walked past with her coffee, making a big deal of avoiding his gaze.

The following Monday, Freda was also a no-show.

"She gave her notice," Rowdy said. "Family business back in Lander. She offered to stay for two weeks, but I told her it wasn't necessary."

Ash felt truly anxious for the first time—Sassy had just been laying low, he thought, taking a few days to herself before returning to the ranch. Trying to give her the space she needed, he slept at the ranch house and buried himself in his work, showing up early and staying until every job was finished. Now he wondered if Sassy had gone to Freda's house.

He had been chomping at the bit to talk with Sassy ever since their blowup. At last, when he was finally able to leave work, he turned towards town, and the bungalow.

Her car wasn't in the driveway, he could tell as he pulled into his own, but the front door was ajar. With his window down, he could hear female voices coming from within the bungalow and felt a surge of hope as he half ran up the stairs to the porch.

"Oh, hello Ash!"

It wasn't Sassy who greeted him, but Casey and her property management team.

"Both girls moved out," she said, matter-of-factly, "we're getting the house ready to rent again. Do you need something?"

"I need..."

I need Sassy.

As Casey held the door open, Ash imagined he could smell a tendril of Sassy's perfume, or a faint waft of her shampoo. It smelled like summer—like Sassy.

I need to go back a few weeks and do everything over again, Ash thought to himself. *I need to tell Sassy that I love her, and that nothing else matters.*

But she was really gone. Ash shook his head sadly and said goodbye to Casey. Like a zombie, he let himself into his house next door and plopped down on a sofa where he fell asleep until late the next morning. Upon waking, his first thought was going to get bagels for Sassy—until he realized where he was, and where she *wasn't.*

Grief and loneliness hit him, and he buried his face in a pillow.

What have I done?

A week later, Ash got up the courage to call Kat. "Have you heard from Sassy; is she alright?"

Kat told him just enough to put his mind at rest, but not his heart.

"Sassy," Kat said simply, "has safely reached her destination."

"Great," he said with a heaviness where his joy used to be.

She went back to Illinois, it seemed, to her mother's house. Ash didn't even know where that was, otherwise he might be tempted to drive through the night to find her.

"Would you... like me to give her a message when she calls, Ash?" Kat's voice was soft and compassionate, he thought.

Tell her I need her; tell her that no place feels like home without her. Tell her that I just might die without her kisses, and that I'm sorry for pressuring her the way I did. Tell her...

"Naw, but thanks," Ash said with a sigh before hanging up.

CHAPTER 57

"Yellowstone reported snow today," Gunnar was sipping coffee at the ranch office, flipping through a local newspaper. Rowdy looked up with interest, but Ash kept his head down as he ate pancakes and link sausage.

He'd worked quietly over the past few weeks, watching summer come to an end.

In Wyoming, the transition from shirt sleeves to jackets happened overnight. Thankfully, Ash kept warm clothing in a locker at the ranch. He was ready for anything. Along the mountainsides, the deciduous trees had changed to a bright yellow, and pops of red and orange could be seen in the underbrush.

While in Michigan, Ash reveled in the change of seasons. But this year, it only served to remind him of the mess he'd made of summer, and of the sweet kisses and golden girl he'd held in his arms, then pushed away in his stubbornness.

"Come visit for the fall colors," Erik had invited the last time they spoke, hoping to cheer up his friend. "We're all going to Charlevoix for a massive bonfire. You and I can sail the big boat to its winter storage location. It'll be a blast."

Ash promised to think about it.

In the meantime, he told Casey to find another renter for his bungalow, because he couldn't bear seeing the happy newlyweds who moved into the house next door to his, where Sassy and Freda spent so many weeks. He also avoided the main house of the ranch and all the family that resided there—especially Kat, who suddenly reminded him of Sassy.

Why had he not seen the resemblance for himself?

He slept in the bunkhouse at night like a seasonal ranch hand and kept to himself during the day. He avoided family gatherings and stayed away from town, and from Amber. Ash knew he owed her an apology and wanted to be sincere and contrite.

She must not be too angry with him, because she'd sent a text only a day or so ago.

"Stop by sometime and see me," she said. "Do some early Christmas shopping."

Christmas! Life was truly moving on, Ash thought, with or without him. Especially if locals were starting their Christmas shopping already.

A WEEK LATER, ASH WEST WALKED DOWN AN EMPTY MAIN STREET IN West Gorge, looking like a man heading to the gallows. An empty soda can lead the way, rolling around in the chill wind. He kicked it a couple of times before picking it up, then tossed it into a recycling bin by the post office.

He sat down heavily on a bench and dropped his head in his hands.

Lifting his eyes, Ash gazed at the town of West Gorge. What he saw was dry pavement and dusty awnings. One or two storefronts sat empty, and a flier for a garage sale flew down the street until it landed under a parked truck.

"Is this the town I gave up love for?" Ash's heart felt dry and cracked under the pain.

Even so, Ash could see that the town wasn't all grim. On the positive side, the main street held Daisy Shire's gallery, the Donut Den, and a small breakfast and lunch diner. The early-rising locals frequented this café before the sun came up most mornings.

There was also the large Mercantile. The window displays were as colorful as they could be as they promoted the functional clothing required in the rugged Wyoming wilderness. Sassy once said they sold shirts that felt like they were made from old tarps.

Ash gave a half smile at the memory—she wasn't far from wrong.

Looking at the town again, Ash saw the Amber Waves store had a steady stream of tourists and locals streaming in and out, carrying shopping bags and laughing at private conversations.

Was Sassy right—should he be with Amber?

It's true that his old high school friend would never leave the town, or the state, or him for that matter. Was that enough? Could they be like couples of old who married based on necessity instead of romance; who poured their energy into taming West Gorge?

Was Amber's willingness enough to make them both happy?

"No, you idiot!"

Ash scolded himself. He knew he'd just be repeating the history he was desperate to avoid. By marrying Amber, he'd create a miserable family because *he* would be miserable. They would splinter apart through bitterness and regret. Ash knew he couldn't possibly give Amber what she desired, and she deserved so much better than a half-hearted, insecure orphan disguised as a worthwhile man.

Hanging his head again, Ash commiserated with the soda can, which was pushed this way and that by invisible forces. He was just as empty and rudderless.

But then, something caught his attention. Voices carrying from Amber Waves that sounded familiar in an unsettling way as words travelled across the road to where he sat. Looking up, Ash's mouth dropped open and he couldn't believe his eyes.

CHAPTER 58

S assy!

Sassy Tate herself, for he'd know her anywhere, stood on the sidewalk in front of the store, and she was talking with—*laughing* with—Amber.

"I like your idea for a display, Sassy," Amber was saying, "we should totally do that."

We?

Ash felt like he was dreaming. For one thing, Sassy left town, didn't she? Weeks ago. Yet here she was in West Gorge. Even more confusing, she was talking with her nemesis, his old friend Amber. The girl Sassy was sure was still in love with him.

Shaking his head, Ash looked again to make sure his eyes weren't playing tricks. The two were gesturing to the storefront and talking together in very friendly tones. As they walked back inside, Ash's guts felt like he'd swallowed a stone, and his heart beat wildly.

Sassy was still here... but why? Why hadn't she let him know?

With legs like iron, Ash tried to remember how to walk as he made his way across the street. His heart beat wildly, and he didn't know what he'd say when he reached the store, only, he had no other choice but to pursue the beautiful golden girl who'd gone inside.

"Oh, hi Ash," Amber said, nearly walking into him on the sidewalk. "I see you got my text. Did you come to do some shopping?"

"No… I came to see…" Ash faltered miserably until Amber put him out of his misery.

"If you're looking for Sassy," she said softly, "she's up the stairs to the right. She's renting from me—apartment B. Go on up."

"But, how long has…" Ash's head was still spinning at the discovery.

"A few weeks," Amber said coolly. "Now if you'll excuse me, I've got customers."

Ash gulped and nodded.

"Thank you, Amber," he said, moving towards the store. Towards the back, there was an old oak door with a sign that read Private. He walked through and saw a staircase leading to the second floor. Taking the stairs two at a time, he reached apartment B and knocked with a trembling hand.

"Just a minute," Sassy's unmistakable voice resonated. When she opened the door, she gave out a quiet gasp at the tall cowboy who stood in the hall, with hat in hand.

Sassy was barefoot, wearing faded jeans with rips at the knee, and a bleached white tee shirt half-tucked and half hanging over the waistline. Her only adornment was her yellow, hair that draped over her shoulder and down her back. She was the most beautiful sight Ash had ever seen.

He wanted to blurt out every thought and apology he'd had since she left, but she beat him to the punch by inviting him in.

"Come in and sit down, Ash," she said.

"I thought you left West Gorge," he said, hearing the croak in his voice.

"Would you like a cup of coffee? I just made a fresh pot—I thought you were Amber coming to grab a cup."

"Um, sure," Ash said. He had a million questions for Sassy, and not the least of which was when… *how* had she and Amber become so chummy?

With shaking hands, Ash took the hot mug from Sassy, who sat across from him. The cup burned his hand but he couldn't take his eyes off of her long enough to set it down.

"I did leave West Gorge, but then I came back. I checked in on my mother then I came back. Kat said I could stay at her condo for as long as I want, but I really need my own place. I answered an ad for an apartment and it was this place," Sassy held her hands up and indicated the cozy room with the tall street-side windows, "and Amber is the landlord."

Sassy smiled and shrugged, and Ash was speechless.

"Turns out," Sassy said with a smile, playfully tossing a throw pillow at Ash, "she and I get along just fine without you in the middle, muddling things up."

"I'm just... forgive me but..." Ash stumbled, "I'm so surprised to see you. My heart just about broke when you left without saying goodbye."

Sassy's smile faded.

"*My* heart broke too, Ash, when you were so angry with me about my secret."

"I was wrong, Sassy."

Sassy looked at Ash for a long while, then spoke as if she hadn't heard what he said.

"As it so happens, Kat, my sister, wants to spend time with me. Imagine that."

"Oh wow," Ash started to say, "that's really great."

She told him how she and Kat spoke every day after their lunch at the condo, and how Kat's heart was softening towards her—something she wasn't sure would ever happen. Even her mother, Sassy said, encouraged her to come back.

"Can you believe that?" Sassy asked.

Ash struggled to get his footing. He never expected to see Sassy when he came to town, or talk with her face to face. He also didn't imagine that they'd be talking about Kat. But Kat is what brought Sassy to West Gorge in the first place.

"So, you came back for Kat," Ash said. His heart ached with

sadness. He felt like a stone had replaced his heart and was pounding away in his bruised chest.

"I came for Kat."

Sassy got up from her chair and moved over to sit by him on the sofa—no doubt to ease the pain of her blunt words, he thought.

"The first time I came to West Gorge, I came for Kat," she continued. "But I came back for you, Ash. For us. To give us a real chance to get to know each other. With no secrets between us."

Tentatively, she reached over and placed a hand on one of his own. She began to pull it away when he didn't respond, but he grabbed it in time and held tight. Tears rolled down Sassy's cheeks and she struggled to finish what she was saying. Ash took her other hand and moved closer to her.

"I thought you might like to know that I'll be here, in Wyoming, at least until Christmas, maybe longer. The accountants that handle West Ranch offered me a job, and the offices are right in town."

Ash leaned over and gently kissed away a tear from her cheek.

"Also," Sassy said as Ash kissed the other cheek, "I told Amber I'd help her through the busy holiday season."

Ash kissed her forehead.

"Plus, I want to stick around for Freda's December wedding to James Timothy." "There's only one problem with that..." Sassy said with half a smile, looking up into Ash's eyes.

"What's that, cowgirl?" Ash continued to kiss her face, then whispered into her ears.

"I... don't have a date, and I hate going to weddings alone."

"Well, I don't know," Ash drawled with a tease in his voice, "I try not to make plans so far in advance. But I'll see what I can do."

At that, Sassy let out a surprised laugh. That's when Ash wrapped both arms around her waist and pulled her close, kissing her full on the mouth with salty tears still on his lips.

CHAPTER 59

*W*hen Sassy's tears had turned to laughter, thanks to Ash's kisses, his phone rang.

"Excuse me, I should take this," he said, and then, "hello... oh, uh huh... yep... uh huh." He stole a sideways glance at Sassy, and handed her the phone. "It's for you."

Skeptical, she took the phone and spoke tentatively.

"Hello?"

On the other end, Kat greeted her.

"Sassy, good, I was hoping to catch you. Are you settled in?"

"Just about, thanks for asking."

Sassy could hear the warmth in Kat's voice, and longed to be with her.

"Perfect. I want to plan a dinner."

"Oh, at the condo again?" Sassy was remembering their lunch at Kat's place in town.

"No, Sassy, at the ranch," Kat said. "It's a *family* dinner, and everyone will be there, I hope. Especially you, my guest of honor."

Sassy had a catch in her throat and held her hand to her trembling lips.

"You've met everyone, but I want to introduce my little sister properly."

All Sassy could do through her tears was nod, which Kat couldn't see, of course. Ash gently took the phone from her hands and spoke.

"She says *Yes*, Kat," he said. "She wouldn't miss it for the world."

END

* * *

KEEP READING FOR FREE BOOK OFFERS, THE NEXT CHAPTER IN ASH AND Sassy's love story, and more from Kathy Fawcett.

WILL ASH AND SASSY'S LOVE STORY GET WRAPPED UP IN A NICE PACKAGE with a pretty bow?

Find out in *Christmas at West Ranch,* coming soon. There's a wedding being planned on the ranch, but who is the bride? Can the big event possibly come off without a hitch? Catch up with the West family as they celebrate the Christmas season together. There will be stolen kisses, sleigh rides, surprises and snow!

READY FOR MORE OF THE WEST BROTHERS ROMANCE SERIES? READ *HER Unexpected Cowboy* free!

She was looking for a cowboy, not a nerd. Then a dangerous bull moose reveals a cowboy heart beating in the chest of this city slicker.

Jaycee's aunt thinks she should broaden her horizons beyond the dusty cowboys she normally dates. But her aunt's latest set-up with Josh, a nerdy city-boy doctor, is way outside her comfort zone. He's nothing like the rough and tumble men she's normally attracted to... until they have a run-in with a rogue moose, and Josh shows Jaycee that being a true cowboy is about a lot more than wearing pointy boots and a hat.

Click here to download your free story, or go to KathyFawcett.com

READ ALL THE BOOKS IN THE WEST BROTHERS ROMANCE SERIES

HER QUARANTINED COWBOY

West Brothers Romance #1

Their blind date is a disaster, and both are happy it's cut short. But a virus forces Kat to lock down the hospital—with Gunnar inside. He hates being stuck anywhere, with anyone. And thanks to a life of privilege, he's been able to call his own shots. But Dr. Kat is the new sheriff in town, and she won't let him bend the rules. Forced to work together, anger turns to admiration, which turns to romance. Can it last when the quarantine is over?

DRAWING HER COWBOY

West Brothers Romance #2

Beautiful and rich, Paislee has a perfect life—or is her controlling fiancée smothering her? Her grandmother suggests a road trip to unravel a family mystery, and she jumps at the chance. But Paislee finds more than she bargained for when she follows cowboy Pike West to an old settler's barn. Trapped by a blizzard, Paislee is soon wearing a prairie dress and dining by candlelight with the cowboy who caught her imagination. Will he catch her heart, too?

STIRRING HER COWBOY

West Brothers Romance #3

Colton West is expecting Chef "Lou" to arrive at the ranch, but he's caught off guard when the beautiful Chef Liu Chen arrives instead. This Asian beauty is a no-nonsense cook who feeds his bottomless appetite, while stirring Colton's desire for love and romance. But Liu has ambitious goals, and a very protective Chinese family. In this conflict of cultures, can Liu keep the cowboy at arm's length? Or will Colton win over the Chen family, and Liu's heart?

HER SUNSET COWBOY
West Brothers Romance #4

After her lowlife ex took everything, Casey Parks rebuilds her real estate empire in small town West Gorge, Wyoming—and she does so with a vengeance. Until her ambition collides with Ridge West, town legend, billionaire, and major thorn in her side. Has the handsome widower set his sights on her territory, or on Casey herself? Time will tell—something Casey and Ridge are running out of during a gripping mountain rescue. In the end, who will rescue who?

SASSY COWGIRL KISSES
West Brothers Romance #5

Sassy is hired for an internship at West Ranch. Arriving with more than a suitcase, she brings a bombshell of a secret that she expects will rock the West family to its core. What she doesn't expect is tall and handsome Ash West. The young cowboy was very good at getting her out of scrapes, distracting her, and kissing her the way no man ever had. Is this just the magic of a Wyoming summer? Or do Ash and Sassy have something worth fighting—and forgiving—for?

CHRISTMAS AT WEST RANCH
West Brothers Romance #6

Will Ash and Sassy's love story get wrapped up in a nice Christmas package? Find out in *Christmas at West Ranch*. There's a wedding being planned on the ranch, but who is the bride—and will the event come off without a hitch? Catch up with the West family as they celebrate the Christmas season together. There will be sleigh rides, more than one surprise, and of course, snow!

OTHER BOOKS BY KATHY FAWCETT

Shoulder Season
Lake Michigan Lodge #1

Kay is finally renovating her lodge and her life. Now who will she share it with? In this funny uplifting tale of renovation, redemption and romance, a rustic old lodge on Lake Michigan isn't the only thing that gets a second chance.

Water Dance
Lake Michigan Lodge #2

Can Kay's happy-ever-after survive an invasion of teenage girls? When Kay agrees to hosting her two nieces for the summer, there's a lot she doesn't know—like, where pretty girls are, boys are sure to follow.

ABOUT THE AUTHOR

Kathy Fawcett is the author of sweet romantic comedy and women's fiction that will keep you smiling, crying and turning pages long past your bedtime. Kathy's funny dialogue and heartfelt stories make her a favorite with a growing number of fans. They love the true-to-life situations, happy endings and highly satisfying sequels. Kathy transports readers to the surf, sand and snow of charming Lake Michigan towns, as well as the windswept mountains of Wyoming.

Home is Michigan, where Kathy worked for years as an advertising writer. She met and married her husband Steve while students at Northern Michigan University, and he introduced her to his home state of Wyoming. Together, they reside near the Great Lakes with their bossy cat Sam, and are surrounded by grown children, grandchildren, and towering pine trees. Stay in touch with Kathy's latest books and projects at kathyfawcett.com where you can also find free stories, or email the author at kathy@kathyfawcett.com